The Way of Things

The Trail of the Crawford Sisters, Volume 1

Emma Rose Lee

Published by Emma Rose Lee, 2022.

THE WAY OF THINGS

First edition. November 1, 2022.

ISBN: 979-8215453865

Written by Emma Rose Lee.

Table of Contents

Chapter 1

Holly

Dust clouds hover over the horizon. There's nothing around for miles but flat land and grass that waves with the wind created by the many wagons as they go by. In my mind, I imagine this is what the sea might look like.

I'm always daydreaming. I'm told that a practical girl shouldn't do such things, that one could wind up in a lot of trouble, but I have yet to walk into a hole and break my neck or step into a den of snakes. Daydreaming is the only thing that keeps me sane in the crazy life I've been tossed into.

I was adopted as a young girl at the tender age of three. I remember nothing about my life before then, but I've been told that I looked as if I'd lived among wild animals. Grass and dirt clung to me, and no one knew what color my skin was until they scrubbed me down in the creek.

At first, I was only referred to as 'The Girl.' The couple who found me in the bushes didn't really see fit to give me a name. It was the older woman, Grandmama, the mother of the wife, who called me Holly because they found me under a holly bush. The name seemed to stick, and as I got older, I was always called Holly.

But I am a misfit, and everyone knows it. Pale skin, freckles, and hair as red and wavy as the campfire flames that glow at night. Many people in our old town thought of me as odd, and odd isn't a good thing where we lived. No one had red hair. Only brown, blond, and black... never too black, or someone would accuse you of being an Indian.

Me? Well, let's just say some people thought I was the devil's child. Grandmama told me to never listen to them. She told me stories of people with hair the color of mine. Of grassy, rolling hills and bagpipes. That I came on a ship from Scotland.

Can you be homesick for a place you've never been to?

My adopted Ma and Pa already had a daughter named May, and she enjoyed holding it over my head that she was the favored daughter. I never held a grudge as it was the way of things. I knew I was Grandmama's favorite, and that was enough.

The captain of our group interrupts my daydreams, shouting that it's time to make camp. The sky is already turning amber. How many miles have we ridden today?

My family had joined a train alongside our neighbors and their son Adam. When we reach Oregon, Adam is to become my husband, and I have no say in the matter, as this is also the way of things.

May told me she was happy it wasn't her who was marrying Adam Saunders. We'd all heard of his father, who was very cruel to his wife. The apple never falls far from the tree.

I jump from the wagon before it stops moving.

"Holly!" Ma scolds from beside the wagon, where she walks with May. We've been taking turns riding on the bench so we each get a break, but it doesn't seem to matter. We're all so tired. Poor Grandmama is laid up in the back of the wagon, battling all the many bumps and pans swinging on their hooks. She said she didn't care anymore. She was too tired to try. The rest of us wouldn't dare ride inside.

"We're only a day and a half ride away from the nearest fort," Pa says to Ma.

The news doesn't excite me as it does everyone else. There's nothing to see but tall, wooden walls and stinky men. Occasionally, the forts we've visited would have a prisoner—a straggling Indian. I would always look away. Soldiers were never kind to anyone unless their skin was white, and even then, it depended.

"I can't go on much longer," Grandmama grouses. I help her out of the wagon. It's shocking how much the woman has aged since we left Missouri three months prior, and it scares me to think about how many months we have left to travel. Will she even be with us then? She's getting up there in age, and her clothes hang off her thin frame. She's whittling away in front of everyone, and no one seems to notice except me.

The trail is hard on everyone. In three months, we've gone from forty families to twenty. The others either went back whence they came or died from the elements.

Our nightly routine begins. Pulling supplies out of the wagons, unhitching teams, leading the livestock to water, feeding and hobbling them, and then feeding ourselves.

Adam comes over after supper to talk to my Pa. He also talks to me, but he found in our early engagement that my Pa is much easier to converse with. I never have much to say to him. I never did. What was I to say? I didn't know him except from what I heard from May. I didn't want to know him any better, if I'm to be honest.

Somewhere in my childish dreamland, I envision I wouldn't be made to marry him, and Grandmama and I would have our own cabin. Even though I know the truth, it's still easier to dream than to think about the now.

"Holly, please help your sister clean up the plates." Ma peers over from the wagon seat.

"Yes'm." I take a place beside May, picking up the soap cake and making a lather in a bucket of creek water. We wash in silence, hearing Adam's and our Pa's plans for when we reach Oregon. I don't listen, but May does. It seems they're always talking about when we get to Oregon. It doesn't seem like we ever will.

"You know, he seems to care for you," May says.

"You're the one that said he would be mean like his Pa."

"Maybe he won't, but you know Pa wants to be rid of you. Ma is expecting by Christmas."

With a new mouth to feed, I would be one too many. I'm only sixteen, hardly a woman, but not a child either.

I don't have to wonder if Adam is mean. I can see it in his eyes every time I refuse to walk with him during the day. He doesn't like being refused, but refused he is.

We finish without another word.

The next day at noon, Pa threatens to toss Grandmama out of the wagon because she wants to stop. Her joints are aching more than usual, but she's too feeble to walk alongside the other women.

"I can't go any farther, Matthew," Grandmama insists once more.

Pa grinds his teeth, and just as he's about to spout out another word to his senile mother-in-law, a cabin appears on the horizon. An abandoned homestead. Pa quickly clamps his mouth shut in shock. It's like God just put it there just for us to find.

"Well, glory be! The Lord be praised!" Grandmama sticks her head out of the wagon just as it comes to a stop.

"Mama, please, stay in the back. It might not be safe," Ma chastises.

The other wagons come to a complete standstill at the sighting of the cabin. Captain Tollier says someone had tried to make a home here and decided they weren't suited for such a hard life.

Grandmama is sure the abandoned cabin is a godsend. Only Pa and the others aren't so sure. I'm not sure what I think.

"If the old woman wants to stay here for a day or two," Captain Tollier says, "I don't see the harm if nothing is amiss. This is a relatively safe area, and Fort Stellar is only a half day away. We'll rest there, and you can come back to get Mrs. Summit."

I'm surprised they agree with Grandmama staying in this abandoned cabin. There's a reason the previous family left.

"I'll stay with her," I insist, and for a second, no one argues against it.

Adam is the first. "I don't like the idea. You shouldn't stay here alone."

"It will be fine." I give him no room for argument. It's decided. I ignore his disdainful stare.

Grumbling about the extra work and lost time, Pa gathers things we'll need and, to my alarm, shoves a pistol into my hand. "Just in case." Then he tells me he's also leaving a horse.

I take the pistol with trembling fingers and do something I haven't done since I was a little girl. I wrap my arms around him and hug him. He pats my head. "You take care, Holly Berry." I smile at the nickname.

"I will, Pa." I turn to follow Grandmama, Ma, and May into the cabin. Pa disappears with a few of the men to poke around the barn and surrounding area and make sure everything is safe.

Whoever left this cabin was in a hurry and left all their furniture and belongings, but it's been so long cobwebs and dust coat everything.

A hearth takes up almost half of a wall, and two rocking chairs face it. A set of chairs and a table are placed on a rag rug behind them. In the center of the table is a vase of dried wildflowers, their petals faded to brown. In the back of the cabin is a bed with a trundle. I immediately stash the pistol directly underneath. Nothing fancy but all functional. It will suit our temporary stay well.

Grandmama looks paler in the cabin, and she collapses into a rocker. Her shoulders slump in fatigue. I worry she's coming down with something. There was a fever going around the train. Everyone that I knew of who had contracted it died. I shake off the thought. We haven't been around anyone who had it.

I get to work, dusting and sweeping everything right out the front door. May attempts to wipe what dust she can off of the table and counters. Ma wraps a blanket around Grandmama's shoulders and kisses her brow. "We'll be back before you know it, Ma." She looks like she might burst into tears. Nothing is certain out here in the wilderness.

"I love you," Grandmama says. "Take care." She gives May a hug, who tears up. I can tell my sister also doesn't think it's a good idea to leave us.

Ma swallows me up in a hug. "You take care as well." My parents and I have never been a real hugging bunch, so this much affection is almost foreign to me.

"I will." I give her a smile, and she leaves the cabin with one last look at us.

THE WAY OF THINGS

May steps in front of me, and at first, I think she's going to pass me on her way out, but she turns to me. "I'll see you soon. Take care, little sister." She draws me into a small hug. "Despite our differences, I love you." The words come out of her mouth rather awkwardly, and she gives a little cough as if to clear her throat, but I know she was trying not to cry. I smile and hug her back. "You too, May." She follows Ma out, and for once, I believe she meant her words.

I watch until the last of the wagons depart, leaving a haze of dust in their wake. I cough and turn away, and Grandmama watches me as I set the dry, rotted broom against the wall, excusing myself to find a new dress to pull over my head. I've been wearing the same dress for over a week, and there's so much dust and stain that I can't see the gingham anymore. To my annoyance, all I find in my little trunk is the wedding dress, tucked in the corner, waiting for its day when we get to Oregon. It's Adam's mother's dress, who came from a well-off family. The dress is beautiful but not practical, but it would have to do for now. With a sigh, I pull it on and button it up.

"Come sit down, child." Grandmama tips her head toward the empty rocker the moment I walk back in. I fall into it, weary and sore. I haven't sat in a real chair in months.

We sit in silence for a while, and then she speaks. "I'm not getting any younger, Holly." Her voice shakes, and I look up at her in surprise. Her blue eyes stare back at me, cloudy and far away, as if she's not really seeing me. Again, I'm worried about her.

"Grandmama, don't talk like that. You still have some years ahead of you." I reach for her hands and squeeze them.

"One never knows when the good Lord will call us home." She smiles at me, but she's as serious as a heart attack.

"I know." I smile back.

"Promise me now that you won't marry the Saunders boy when you get to Oregon. He's got bad blood, that one. You're so pretty in that dress, and he won't appreciate you for you. I know his Pa."

My fingers clench the lace of my dress. She's never spoken of my future marriage before; always keeping her place as the silent one in the house, even though she was always more of my mother than Ma herself, and everyone knew it. Ma had baby May when I came along and had little time for another little one. Grandmama took me under her wing almost immediately. She's always been my constant. Her talk of not getting any younger spooks me. Finally, I find my voice. "I would very much like to find my own way—" I stumble across my words. "I mean my own choice of husband." My cheeks redden.

"Don't be like your Ma and Pa."

I know exactly what she means. My parents had a marriage of convenience right from the start. There was no love, and there never will be, but thankfully, my Pa is not a violent man.

"I may not be here to see you fulfill your promise, but I'll be watching."

"Grandmama!" Now she's really scaring me.

She simply shakes her head. "My time is coming, darling. I can feel that this is my last and final stop. That was why I insisted on staying here and not going ahead."

I block out her words from my heart, not wanting to listen to such talk, but I'd suspected she might not be around to see our final destination. I say nothing and simply shake my head, feeling a lump forming in my throat and swallowing it back with a smile.

THE WAY OF THINGS

After our talk, I check on our horse, Dusty, and then come back to cook beans in the hanging pot. I can almost forget our little conversation.

In the night, my worst fears come true, and I remember her warning.

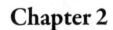

Chapter 2

Holly

I wake up the next morning shivering in the trundle bed. The fire in the hearth has long since died out, and I'm thankful that the family who left had chopped-wood ready beside the fireplace.

I'm just about to get up and revive the flames when a cough rattles above me.

"Grandmama, are you all right?" I peek up at her, but she doesn't answer. She still sleeps, but fitfully. Beads of sweat dot across her wrinkled forehead.

Blinking the rest of the sleep from my eyes, I jump up from the bed and lean over her, touching her forehead. I yank my hand back, a terrified lump forming in my throat. No... it's the fever. Not sure what to do, I stand there dumbly, looking down at the deathly-sick woman in the bed. My vision tunnels, and I fight to stand straight. It's like it's not me standing there; that I'm just there watching someone else. There is no doctor and no medicine. Only me. I can't let my emotions take over. I have to think about what to do.

I tuck the blanket around Grandmama. Gingerly, I reach under my mattress and pull the gun out, stepping quickly to place it on the table and treating it like it's a stick of dynamite. I stumble back to restart the fire then pull my boots on.

THE WAY OF THINGS

There's a wide expanse of trees around the cabin and, somewhere, there are bound to be medicinal herbs waiting for me to find them. Better yet, there might be white willow bark.

I look at the frail woman in the bed behind me and steel myself. I don't want to leave her here by herself, but I know I must for her own good. For my own good.

The pistol Pa gave me glints on the table, and I hesitantly grab it and tuck it into the satchel that I take with me everywhere. "I will be back, Grandmama," I vow and step out of the cabin. No turning back now. I walk straight and tell myself not to look back.

Unease works its way through me as I walk deeper and deeper into the dense wood. If I keep walking, I'll soon be lost. The ground is more barren than it should be, almost as if there was a fire recently. Is that the reason that the family abandoned the cabin?

I grab sparse sprigs of random herbs as I go along on the search for a white willow. Dry leaves crunch under my feet, and I realize how loud I'm being, but there's no one around aside from myself... at least, I assume. The birds above me sing to each other a few yards ahead, and as I look up, I finally spot a willow. I sprint for it and quickly get to work, dropping the bark into my bag. In my concentration, I fail, at first, to notice there's someone only a few feet from where I stand. Long hair... deerskin leggings... A shriek threatens to bubble out of me, and I cover my mouth, stifling it.

An Indian is crouched down by a tree next to a patch of yellow flowers. I watch as he lifts a flower to his nose. The scene is so tranquil—until he lifts his head and meets my eyes.

A piece of bark slips from my fingers, and I gasp, realizing I've completely stopped and forgotten what I'm supposed to be doing. How dreadful am I?! I blink at him, willing him to look away, but he doesn't, and now we're locked in a staring match. I bend to pick up the bark I dropped, keeping my gaze locked on his. How am I going to escape?

And if that's not the worst of my problems, two bird calls trill in the distance, and the hairs on the back of my neck stand up. Those are not birds. I shrink into myself, holding my breath.

The man with the yellow flower frowns at me, and I frown too. I wonder if he'll let me go quietly or sound the alarm to his friends. He stands up and turns his head toward the so-called birds, releasing me from his stare, and trills back.

I tense, clutching my satchel with all I'm worth. I must get back to Grandmama before it's too late for the both of us.

Looking back, he assesses me with his brown eyes. There's no evil intention in his gaze, and I realize how normal and civilized he seems. Not at all like the imaginations my Pa conjured up with his stories of 'heathen Injuns'. Don't get me wrong. This doesn't mean I'm not scared silly.

He nods at me, and I blink at him in shock. His pleasant face fixes into a scowl when I don't move, and it takes me a second to understand he wants me to leave. He makes a frantic shoo-ing motion at me, repeating the motion several times when all I do is stare up at him.

Another "bird" calls, and this one is even closer. That's all the motivation I need. I spin on my heels so fast that I pitch forward and have to right myself, landing on one hand to propel back into flight. I don't look back, instead running as fast as I can out of these woods, determined never to step foot in them again.

By the time I reach the cabin, I'm shaking from head to toe, but I don't stop to reflect on what just transpired. I grab the bucket by the door after I check on Grandmama once more. She's even more feverish now, and the first needles of real fear settle over me, heightened by my scare in the woods.

I run to the stream behind the cabin. My hands shake so hard that, by the time I get back to the threshold, there's only half a bucket of water left, though I'd filled it to the brim. I can't be bothered to care at this point. I just need a little water, and I don't dare leave the cabin for more.

Setting the bucket down, I slide the latch on the door for good measure. It might not be the toughest door, but having a lock will give me some peace of mind.

I lay out the bark and herbs across the table while the water is heating over the fire. When I've prepared the white willow into tea, it ends up being too hot, and I'm forced to wait before bringing it to Grandmama.

I prop her head up and bring it to her lips, but she barely swallows, letting most of it run out her mouth. Tears pool my eyes as desperation fills me. She's the only genuine family I have in this world. No one knows or cares for me the way she does. What would I do without her? "Grandmama, you must drink it. You have to get better," I plead with her.

A slight wheeze escapes her mouth, and I bend low to make out her words. "Let me..." I frown, listening hard. "Jesus..."

The tears that pooled in my eyes moments before dribble down my cheeks. I don't have to hear anymore to understand that she wants me to let her be—that she's tired of the Oregon Trail. She always said she was too old for this adventure, but Pa hadn't listened to her complaints and dragged her along anyway. Now she's paying the price.

Despite her words, I stay by her side the rest of the day and night, trying to give her sips of broth or the willow bark tea. I hang the other herbs to dry, not sure why I bother since they won't be ready before Pa gets back to me... Us... Perhaps it's nerves, but I have to keep myself busy, or I know I'll fall into a dark place.

Howls and wails filter through the rickety cabin door that night, and my hand never strays far from Pa's pistol. The noises sound more human than animal. Coyotes and wolves can't open the door, but Indians can, and I can't shake myself from thinking about the Indian with the yellow flower who'd let me go before his friends had seen me. Just because one Indian seemed of a nice sort didn't mean the others wouldn't scalp me at first sight. As I grip the wooden handle of the gun, I pray that we both survive the night.

Some time later, I must have fallen asleep, because when I open my eyes, light beams crawl their way under the door. I jerk to my feet in horror. The pistol clatters down from my skirt and falls on top of the cold cup of tea beside me, busting it into a million tiny pieces. The noise is louder than a gunshot, and I am now fully awake because the cabin is too quiet and much too cool.

And I know of one thing. I'm now very much alone.

Chapter 3

Holly

I take much too long to gather my bearings before I step over the broken cup to get to the trundle bed. "Grandmama?" My voice shakes as badly as my hands. I know she won't answer.

She is too still. Her white hair frames her weathered face, and her eyes are looking up as if she can see something I cannot.

I should be happy that she's free, but instead, I crumble to my knees and cry for the closest person I had to a mother. Awareness creeps over me. I'm alone in this cabin, and the wilderness is all around me. The wagon train is gone, and Pa hopefully will come for me in the morning, but doubts tease me. What if Pa and Ma decide I'm not worth coming back for? Pa already wanted to get rid of Grandmama, and if he left me, he would have one less mouth to feed. Especially with the new baby coming.

I gulp and shake myself. Those kinds of thoughts are not a good idea. I need to get up and quit feeling sorry for myself, and go find a shovel and a good place to dig. If I don't start now, it will be dark before I'm done, since I've never done much digging except for gardening.

It's not a good idea to leave a body unburied for more than a day. I'd seen it on the trail.

I stand up and cover Grandmama with the old, dusty quilt she's wrapped in. I can't bear to look at her unblinking eyes anymore.

To my dismay, there is no shovel in the barn or anywhere on the homestead. Giving up, I find a rather sharp-looking stick and dig for all I'm worth between two trees, away from the cabin. I picked a spot close to the creek. It seems fitting.

By noon, I'm hot and feeling sick. I try to tell myself it's the sun, but I'm not so sure.

My digging proves fruitless after a while, and as much as I want to dig six feet, I know I'd be lucky to get to three feet. I resort to digging by hand until my fingers threaten to fall off.

Hours later, I can go no further, and I nearly crawl into the creek to soak my abused hands. The poor, white dress I wear is no longer white, but a dark, mottled gray. I'm sweating but no longer hot. I know I must have caught what Grandmama had, but I can't think about it now. I have to keep moving. I can worry about myself later.

Another two hours later, I drag the body to its final resting place on a roughly made stretcher pulled by Dusty and push dirt back over the hole to fill it. I pile stone after stone on top, hoping and praying it will keep the animals away.

I can no longer cry, sitting there by the pitiful grave. Perhaps I'm too tired. The sickness that took my grandmother is trying to claim me.

At night, I force myself to drink the same tea I made for Grandmama. I stubbornly stay in the rocking chair, wrapped in a blanket. I can't bear to sleep in the same place she died, and I refuse to let myself succumb to this fever. If I lay down, I might never get back up. I'm so tired. I grasp the pistol once more. This place is not safe.

THE WAY OF THINGS

I doze off at some point and snap awake when I hear a howl and a yip, and then another join in.

"No!" I jerk forward, clumsy in my hazy state. Gripping the pistol, I bolt outside toward the noise. I should think more about my safety, but I'm angry that the wolves are trying to defile my Grandmama's grave.

Dusty screams and paws the ground in a frenzy to escape the sight of the wolves, and I watch for only a moment as the rope snaps and my only way to escape this place gallops away to leave me to defend against the wolves.

"Get! Go away!" I scream, waving my arms. The wolves keep digging and snuffling. There are five in total, and three step forward, locking their golden gazes on me as if to ask what I'm doing interrupting their meal.

What am I doing? I should go back... but I can't let them have my grandmother's body.

Shakily, I lift the pistol with two hands and take aim. Bile fills me as I pull the trigger and watch as one of the mangy animals drops to the ground in a heap. That's when I notice I only have one bullet left. I aim at the closest animal, but my hand is trembling and I miss, giving the two wolves closing in on me an advantage.

The clicks of the empty gun seem louder than the gunshots.

"No..." I plead, taking a step back in alarm.

That's all the encouragement these wolves need.

I drop the pistol and try to run.

Stillwater

I'd seen plenty of the white people's wagons go through our lands. It was always a curious thing. Hundreds of funny, white-covered, wooden contraptions dotting the ground. It never failed to amaze me how anyone thought going across a mountain with one of those things was possible.

Curiosity got the better of me the day I ran into the red-haired girl who seemed, for all I knew, completely alone, which was odd. No one tries to live by themselves. Especially not a white man or woman.

Curiosity again is the reason I'm walking toward the abandoned homestead. I've investigated this place so many times before. I've seen lots of white families come and go. Staying for only one or two moons at a time. Gone before the next. No one wants to stay. You can't tell a white man his way of living will not work here in our land. They want to tear apart the earth and plant things that will never grow in this much-too-rocky ground.

They won't accept help from my people. If they did, they could flourish in this land. No, instead they want to fight us because they don't understand our ways or even want to try. We're different, and that makes us all a threat to each other. A never-ending circle of misunderstandings and needless killing.

What they should be more frightened of are the wild animals.

THE WAY OF THINGS

Anyone who stays in this strange, wooden wigwam is scared off not by my people, but by the wolf pack that frequents the area.

If the red-haired girl is alone, she could be in danger. She was gathering medicinal plants yesterday. Perhaps she had someone sick she was caring for.

I'm thankful I learned some of the English language during my time away from the village. Now I can talk to her. It was frowned upon, but someone needed to understand. Most everything about me has been frowned upon since the moment I picked up a pestle and mortar instead of a bow and quiver full of arrows. Sure, I knew how to use weapons, but it wasn't on instinct like others in my village.

The chief adopted me as a young boy, and as his son, I was expected to learn from him and become a great warrior. But I just couldn't bring myself to take life. What I wanted most was to learn medicine and help others.

A growl pierces the quiet of the night, and I grip the knife in my belt, pulling it out of its sheath.

"Get! Go away!" someone shouts in English. I break through the clearing just as a gunshot pierces the air. Howls and growls follow its ring, and I'm met with a scream.

A figure races by me; the girl from yesterday. A pistol drops from her hands as she desperately tries to outrun the two wolves coming after her.

I spring into action, catching one wolf by surprise, but my relief is short-lived. Too late to escape danger, the girl falls to the ground, and a wolf catches her leg, prepared to tear it to bits. Only hungry and desperate wolves ever act this unhinged.

She screams, beating at the wolf's head, but it refuses to let go.

I'm too far away to reach them, so I do the only thing I can and pray to the Great Spirit. My mark is true. The blade pierces the wolf in the back of its head. The animal stills, and so does the girl.

She watches me in horror while I remove the knife, wipe it, and kick the wolf carcass over to the side. She must believe I plan to kill her. Funny, since I just saved her life. I turn away to look behind us.

Seeing their comrades fall, the rest of the pack flees the clearing, and now I can see what they were after. A fresh grave. The girl hadn't been alone after all, until now. I look back at her, but she's fallen into a dead faint. It's not only the wolf bite she's ailing from. A sickly pallor covers her fair skin, and sweat coats her as if she's just ran a mile.

If her family member died, it had to be whatever illness plagues her.

What I do next is beyond stupid, but I can't just leave her to die alone, and the cabin is no longer safe.

I take her.

Chapter 4

Stillwater

The closer I get to my village, the more I realize what trouble I'm about to get myself into by bringing a sick white woman home. What else was I supposed to do? I very well couldn't leave her in that cabin. She wouldn't survive longer than a day without proper care and medicine.

She doesn't wake up, no matter how I jostle her around. Not even when I reach my tepee and place her on my own pile of furs.

Healing River peeks his head in, as if he's following me. Probably to see what sick thing I've brought this time. Although I'm better known for bringing sick animals, not people, to my tepee.

"What have you done this time, Stillwater?" he tuts in disapproval. "The people will not like this." He steps inside to peer down at the feverish woman and steps back.

"The only one that matters is my father, who I'm about to talk to about bringing her here. She has no one and would have died if I'd left her in *that cabin*." I turn to the shaman. "Could you please do what you can while I go to my father?"

Healing River doesn't look happy but nods and sets to work. I don't waste time, leaving the girl to the medicine man and praying she doesn't wake up just yet. She would have a scare if she did.

My father, the chief, sits in his tepee by a small fire to ward off the chill in the air. He looks up when I step inside.

"My son. What has brought you here?" His words are friendly, but his gaze is guarded, as if afraid I might bear bad news...

"I have brought a white woman that has lost her family to my tepee. She was attacked by wolves and is ailing from a fever." I don't step too close to him since I'm not sure, just yet, if I will get sick.

"A sick woman?" His tone is the same as Healing River's, but anger also clouds his face. "You are being irresponsible, putting our people in danger for one white woman. It is no doubt she is being plagued by the same sickness that took her family, and you brought her here." He rises from his position by the fire to stand tall over me. I look up at him, trying not to feel like a boy at twenty-four summers.

"I had no choice. I couldn't leave her at that old cabin. She would have died, and I had no way to treat her out there." I know I'm in the wrong, but I couldn't let her die, and he knows it.

Father sighs and rubs at a wrinkle on his forehead. I'm sure I put the wrinkle there myself. In fact, I'm more than sure of it. "You never were one to let anything wounded die. It's in your nature to help others, and I cannot punish that. While this white woman is sick, you must stick to your tepee and keep away from all others except Healing River. I will make sure everyone stays clear, at least for now."

I give him a nod. "Thank you, Father."

THE WAY OF THINGS

"We will talk about what becomes of her later. Just make her well, Stillwater." He steps outside, and I follow to return to my new patient.

Holly

Smoke tickles my nose, and I gasp awake. I try to sit up, but the world is tilting, and I feel like I weigh of lead.

"Easy, do not move," a voice speaks beside me. A male voice with a heavy accent.

I do the complete opposite, jerking forward in another attempt to sit up, and fall back with a yelp of pain. My right leg is on fire. Frantically, my eyes dart around the room—no, tepee.

Whaaat? How did I get—?

"No moving," the exasperated voice tells me, going off into another tongue. Another voice answers back.

I shake my head and force my eyes to move toward the voice, taking in two Indian men. One sports wrinkles and holds a bundle of herbs that are smoking, putting off a calming fragrance... but I don't want to be calm. I want to get up and run and scream.

The younger Indian, the one who told me not to move, is frowning. It's then I realize I know this one. He was in the woods, gathering those yellow flowers. Memories, though foggy, come back to me. I went outside to fend off the wolves at Grandmama's grave, but I'd only had two bullets, so I ran, and one wolf attacked me. The urge to scream claws at my throat. *He* killed the wolf and then came at me—

I give a shriek, despite myself, and attempt to scoot back, but I don't get far.

24

"Stay!" he hisses at me.

The older man with the herbs recoils and curls his lip, but I pay him no mind and keep my full attention on the younger and current threat.

His arms are crossed, and he looks annoyed. I realize now that he had spoken to me in English when, in the woods, he acted as if he couldn't talk.

"You took me away. Why?" The words come out harsh, and I know I sound like an indignant child, but I don't care. I have a right to complain, and I will.

His brow furrows.

The older Indian is back to waving his herbs around, and I cough. The calming scent is choking me, and I wonder if he's doing it on purpose.

"It was no longer safe." His English is fairly clear, and it shocks me further.

My eyes water. I'm not sure if it's from actual tears or the smoke. "My family is coming back tomorrow."

He shakes his head. "Three suns have passed."

"What?!"

"If they have come back, they will think you are dead and gone," he says in a tone one would use with a child. I guess I deserve it with the way I'm handling my situation.

I seethe. "No!" I sit up and try to stand, but the moment I put weight on my foot, it buckles under me and I whimper.

Muttering something under his breath in his language, he grabs me before I fall into a disgraceful puddle, then he eases me back down with gentleness, though his words are biting. "I said stay put!" He glowers at me. "You do speak the white man's words?"

I huff in compliance. There's nothing else I can do. I'm trapped here.

The older man shakes his head, saying something to my captor, and then he leaves with his offending smoke.

I can finally breathe deeply, and I do, though I never once take my eyes off my captor.

"You will stay in this tepee until you can walk on your feet." His words are final, and my shoulders slump in defeat. "It will do you no good to try and crawl outside. You will not get far, and my people will not be kind to you without my protection." He turns away from me to look outside.

His people... My situation is becoming more dire by the second. If it's so dangerous, then why did he bring me here? The wolves would be safer than an entire group of Indians.

"Why are you helping me?"

He looks back at me in surprise. Perhaps because I'm staying put. "You wouldn't have survived another moon out there. A woman alone is not safe."

I frown. I know deep down he's right, but Pa was due to return the very next day. If I hadn't gotten caught up in the wolves' dinner, I would be back with the wagon train. A pang of loneliness flits through me. It wouldn't have been the same there without Grandmama. She'd been my only constant companion. No one else understood me or cared for me like she did... but in the end, they were my people, and I definitely don't belong here. Where do I even belong now? Nowhere... I shake myself before I sink further into my sadness. Feeling sorry for myself will get me nowhere today or tomorrow—or any day, for that matter. This man is my captor, but also my savior. It would be wise to listen to him if I want to survive.

THE WAY OF THINGS

If he wanted me dead, he would have let the wolves have me, but he didn't.

"What's your name?" My words are soft and hesitant. Am I being too bold asking for his name? I should know his name.

His guarded, brown eyes assess me as if he can't figure out what to make of me. "They call me Stillwater."

"My name is Holly," I offer back, meeting his gaze.

He gives me a nod. The guarded expression on his face is less severe, but he still doesn't trust me, and I would say it's fair since I don't trust him either. At least I have a name to put to his face.

My stomach growls, and I blush. Perfect timing... I look away from him to run my fingers through the furs I'm lying on.

I jump when he gives a little laugh. "Hungry?"

"Y-yes, I think so." I still refuse to look up. It's humiliating to be at the mercy of someone you don't even know. All my life, I've always been independent. I'm not used to how this is supposed to work.

"I will get something to fill your hollow belly." He parts the tepee flap and doesn't wait for me to say anything.

"Thank you." My words are said to the open air, and I suddenly feel very alone all over again.

Stillwater

I brace myself for the moment I step outside and don't wait for the fire-haired woman's answer. I can tell that she's not used to being looked after and told what to do, but looking after people is what I do, and I plan to do just that. Even if I have to tie her up to keep her from crippling herself.

Her anger toward me would be wholly justified if I told her the truth about the family she thought abandoned her. I felt wretched not saying a word of it, but with her injured and just over the fever, I didn't think it was right to tell her yet. It would further her opinions toward me and my people. I know she believes us all to be the heathens the white men tell tales about. Perhaps it is true about some of us, but there are also as many white 'heathens' as there are Indian ones. The whites at the fort have acted far worse than animals most of the times I've visited there. I always refused their fire water. I wanted nothing to do with anything that made me act crazy.

A pot of stew is already simmering over a fire. I scoop some into a bowl, hoping that it's at least a little edible. I'm not a cook, but if I expect to feed her—Holly—then I must make her something. None of the women here will give me anything. In fact, the entire village camp is upset that I've dragged a white woman here. It doesn't matter that she's injured and sick with a fever. They're mostly upset, of course, because she is sick, but I'll make sure I keep her isolated in my tepee. If I or anyone else were going to be infected with the fever, we would have gotten it days ago.

Nevertheless, I can feel disapproving eyes boring into me, and it makes me itch. I tell myself not to look up, but against my better judgment, I do... right into the eyes of Rising Sun. She stands on the other side of the fire with her arms crossed.

She narrows her eyes. "You should have left that white woman. Why have you brought her here, requiring you to do the chores of women? This is beneath you, Stillwater."

I try not to scowl. "The women refuse to let her eat their food. How else will she eat?"

Rising Sun grits her teeth. "What will you do when she is well? She can't stay here."

"When the time comes, I will know."

It doesn't seem to appease her, but she closes her mouth and glances toward the tepee where the red-haired woman is. She hasn't come near Holly yet for fear of her sickness, but now that she is well, I expect she will come see the white woman for herself.

I'm not sure what will happen to Holly when she is well enough to take care of herself. She can't live on her own, and her people are long gone. The truth of the matter is she has no one unless she waits for the next wagon train, which might not be before the next snow. All she has is my people, and they refuse to have her. I know I've dug my own grave, and I also know I'll continue to dig deeper before this is all over.

I don't wait for Rising Sun to say another word and, instead, turn back to the tepee with my bowl of meager deer stew. One day, she will get over her hatred of white people. Everyone assumes I will take her as my wife soon, but it is hard to imagine. I don't want a wife that doesn't understand me and my need to help others. Few try to understand me, but that's how it is for an adopted son.

Holly

I shift on my elbow and try to keep from brushing my sore leg against the furs. Now that I'm more alert, it's hurting even more. It makes me wince just to think what it might look like under the bandage. I will most undoubtedly have a scar to remind me for the rest of my life.

A woman's voice rises in anger outside the tepee, and I jump in surprise. Stillwater answers in a quiet voice, but there's a hint of anger around the edges. He doesn't like what she's saying. What is she saying? Now I wish I could understand their language.

I frown, almost sure it was about me. That would make one of his people angry, I would think. That older man with the herbs definitely didn't like me being here. Well... I don't like being here either. Not that I have any choice in the matter. Even if I could walk away, where would I even go? I have no one and nowhere to be. My best bet would be to go towards the fort that was a day's ride away, but even I know it isn't a place for a lone woman to go. If I happened to make it, the only thing for me to do would be to marry a man who needed a wife. A loveless, miserable marriage. The same thing that would happen if I found my wagon train. I have a bad feeling that I'll never see my family again. I am lost to them.

The tepee flap opens, and I watch Stillwater enter with a bowl made of bone. Its contents swirl steam in dancing circles. My stomach gives another growl as if to greet him, and I turn red once more.

Stillwater squats beside me and sets the bowl down. I flinch when he places his hands on my back but relax as he helps me sit up. I don't know what to make of him. He's so civilized for a 'heathen'. More civilized than the men I had to endure on the trail.

Once I'm propped up, he hands me the bowl and sits back. He plans to watch me eat. I'm much too hungry to care and put the bowl to my lips. The smell is pleasant, at least. I take a sip and, aside from being a bit bland, it's delicious. I tip it up more, and before I know it, the bowl is empty. Stillwater is still assessing me quietly, like a doctor would a patient. Is he a doctor to his people? It would make sense, since he's tending to me.

"Thank you."

He takes the bowl from me and gives me a nod. Something he seems to do a lot.

"We should redress your wound," he tells me, standing up and crossing to the other side of the tepee.

My heartbeat picks up in tempo. "It burns."

"As it should. You were bitten and nearly lost your leg." Stillwater comes back holding new wraps and a container of some funny, brown paste.

His words turn my stomach, and I don't want to see what's under that bandage. But once more, I have no choice in the matter.

He sits back down beside me, and I watch him, adjusting the skirt away from my bulky bandage. He unwinds the cloth quickly, as if he's done this many times.

I can't help myself and look away. I wince as the air hits my leg, and Stillwater says nothing as he continues with his task. I yelp at the coldness of the paste and regret it when I look back.

Yep... those are teeth marks.

I gulp.

"Be brave, and be grateful that you still live," Stillwater says quietly, taking the new wraps and winding them around my leg until the bite marks disappear, and I relax. I've never been very good with blood or wounds, and definitely not my own.

Even though I'm still upset that he took me away, I feel gratitude that he saved me from those wolves. If he hadn't been there, I would have surely died. The words come out of my mouth in a croak. "Thank you."

He looks up at me. Those eyebrows furrow again. "You are angry I took you, but you thank me anyway for it?" He ties the bandage in a knot at the top and changes the subject. "It's healing well."

My face burns in shame. What is it about this man that makes me feel this way? I have every right to be angry... I do, and yet now I feel ashamed for it. He's done nothing but help me all this time while I was oblivious to the world.

"I'm angrier at being left alone by my family, but I am thankful to be alive." I try to explain myself.

"They didn't leave you alone. They thought you were dead and had no reason to stay," Stillwater insists.

"Did you hear of them coming back?" Surely he had, since he was out in those woods that time.

"No, and my people have seen no white men coming this way in a while." His words make me nervous. What if Pa had never come back for me and was willing to leave me behind with Grandmama? An awful coldness settles inside me, freezing my insides.

Stillwater stands up and puts away his tools. I notice he avoids my eyes. Does he know something he's not telling me about my family? The thought has me feeling paranoid, but I stuff it back into the corner of my mind.

"How long do I have to stay here?" By here, I mean the tepee and pile of furs.

"When you can put weight on your leg again, then you can go outside." He frowns, and I feel he doesn't like the idea of me going outside any more than I like the idea of staying holed up inside.

"I'll have to practice then."

"No, you will stay." He shakes his finger at me like I'm a dog, and I glower. My mood slips once more. "No one will bother you here. No one lives here but me," he promises as if it might make me feel better.

After a while, he leaves me once more, and the time passes by slowly, but sometime before the sun sets, I fall asleep.

Howls fill the air, and I tell myself not to look behind me. I run.

I'm surrounded, but I have to get to Grandmama's grave. They're digging it up, and I have to stop them before it's too late. I won't let them have her! I can't!

I lift the pistol in my hand and point it at the wolf closest to me. The shaggy beast drops to the ground, but the other two beside it stop digging to stare at me. I take a wary step back. I shouldn't have done that.

There's a growl behind me, and I whip around in horror. There's no time to react. No time to lift the gun again and shoot. I hit the ground on my back, and gray fur blurs in front of me.

The wolf that had stalked me from behind pins me to the dirt. I recoil from its foul breath, fangs extended close to my face. My hand still grips that pistol, and I point it up, cock it, and pull the trigger. It gives a funny, little click, and my stomach drops in horror.

There are no more bullets...

Drool drips from the animal's jowls, and I tremble. The wolf snarls as if he knows he has me now. The other wolves gather closer as if to watch us.

I may not survive this, but I refuse to die lying down, so I do the only thing I know to do. I slam the pistol into the wolf's face. He yelps like a kicked puppy and jolts away from me. For just a second, I am free. I don't waste any time and roll away. I'm on my feet again and running in the opposite direction, and, for a minute, I feel like I'm going to make it. Just a few strides from the cabin. Something yanks me back, slamming me to the ground face first.

Teeth dig into my leg, and I know that it's over. I'm being dragged away.

Something brushes against my arm, drawing me away from the darkness behind my eyelids... away from this awful dream that I will dream again.

I struggle to open my eyes and look up at the intrusion, but my eyelids are so heavy that it seems almost impossible.

The brushing grows harder before turning into a sharp poke. The heaviness is lifted from my eyes in an instant, and they fly open.

A figure hovers above me. An unfamiliar female. She stares down at me in disdain with her almond-shaped eyes. She pokes me again, and I realize that the Indian woman is holding a stick and is prodding me with it.

I scream and scoot away, making my leg sear in another bout of pain. I didn't mean to cry out, but I couldn't keep it at bay. The noise jerks the woman back, and she shrieks right along with me, pointing the stick out like a spear. Words spew out of her mouth.

That foreign tongue spoken by Stillwater and his people. She must be one of them as well. What is she doing in Stillwater's tepee?

I shake my head, hoping she will understand that I don't know what she's saying. Unfortunately, that makes her talk that much faster, and she flails her arms at me as if I'm the most unintelligent creature she's ever set eyes on. I can tell she doesn't like me and wants me to go away. Is she any relation to Stillwater? His sister or his betrothed? She must be someone important for her to act this way.

The tepee flap slaps back quickly and Stillwater is inside, alarm filling his face at the sight of my pallor skin, and then he looks toward the intruder in annoyance. I sit back and watch as the two have it out with each other. It could be almost comical if I understood what they were saying, and it didn't revolve around me. I don't like being the center of attention, especially this kind.

The woman points the stick at me and yells at Stillwater in outrage. I'm beginning to think she isn't his sister, but in fact, his betrothed. I don't really want to be in the middle of a love spat, but as fate would have it, and my mutilated leg, I wasn't going anywhere. Not at all.

Stillwater just shakes his head in exasperation. He points toward the entrance and says one word. I'm almost sure it was 'leave,' but she's not paying attention to him and continues to rant on without a care.

She turns toward me, still pointing with her stick. Once more, she pokes me in the side with it, and I wince away from her jabs. She says something to me, and I can tell without even knowing her words that it's a threat. She pulls back her arm as if to strike me, and I brace myself, scooting further away.

THE WAY OF THINGS

Stillwater grabs the hand that's holding the stick and wrenches the offending object away. He looks angry now and yanks the woman away from me, dragging her out of the tepee, raving mad.

Whoever that was, I hope I never see her again, but I have a little feeling I'll be seeing a lot more of her.

Stillwater

I knew I shouldn't have left Holly alone, but I had duties to tend to, and it couldn't be helped. I should have known that Rising Sun would take my absence as a time to study what she called my broken plaything. I didn't think she could be so violent toward another human being. When I walked into that tepee to see her ready to strike my patient, I was more than a little shocked.

I hadn't read the signs of Rising Sun's real dislike for me keeping a female captive. I knew she wanted to marry me, and she felt threatened by another woman's presence. She doesn't understand that I simply helped Holly because she had no hope of surviving if I hadn't. Explaining my reasons would help nothing. Instead, I shunned her away and hurt her pride. Holly has only been here less than seven moons and already made an enemy. This isn't going so well and will probably only get worse.

I'll have to keep my time away from Holly shorter and, when she heals enough to walk, take her with me. There's just no other way around it, at least for her time being here, however long that is to be.

She will never be safe in this village.

Rising Sun stalks away from me in a huff, leaving her lethal, little switch in my hands. I can expect her to give me the silent treatment for a few days. She might think it will bother me, but I'll be glad for it. She has her sights set on me to marry her by the next season. Everyone expects it since she is closer to me than anyone in the village besides my father. I only ever thought of her as a good friend, and she's mistaken it for something else, but her jealousy toward the white woman is unjustified.

Ever since I was old enough to follow Healing River around to learn the trades of a medicine man, I've always helped people. The warriors in the tribe poked fun at me because I'd rather heal a life than kill one. I was not fit to be the chief's son to them. My father wasn't happy with my choice of trade, but, even though I could never be a shaman in name, he allowed me to follow the old man, Healing River, around until I eventually put him out of his trade. He was a grumpy elder, but he understood me, for the most part. This particular patient of mine, he greatly disapproves of, but he isn't the one taking care of her.

This may be the first time in my life I question my reasons for trying to help someone. What was I thinking, bringing a white girl into this village? I need to get her out of here as quickly as possible. Rising Sun won't be the last person ready to harm her.

I scrub my hand across my face in distress, torn between what I am to do about this situation I've gotten myself into.

Holly sits right where I left her, and her face has lost all its color. She looks up at me when I step inside the tepee. Her expression is guarded, untrusting, and I have this feeling that we are back to where we started. Guarded strangers. I should try not to care so much, but I don't like the idea of her being afraid of me or anyone else.

"She doesn't want me here," she says listlessly, sounding as if she's somewhere else.

"Rising Sun will not bother you anymore," I promise.

She doesn't look like she believes my words in the least bit. "You're important to her."

I shake my head. "Friends."

After that, silence follows, and we talk no more about Rising Sun or Holly being at camp.

Chapter 5

Holly

Days pass slowly now that I'm awake, and I'm never allowed out of the tepee.

I wouldn't dare try to go outside by myself, even though I tested my leg a day ago and I could walk on it without too much of a limp. Stillwater has made no promises of letting me venture out in the open.

The days pass in a routine. I stop talking about my situation. It wasn't doing any good anyway, and instead, I ask questions about his people, and he asks me about mine. While he's away, I rest, and when he comes back, we talk about his day, because mine is never all that interesting.

After three days, I can't stand it anymore. I can't stay in this tepee. Stillwater hasn't mentioned a word about letting me go out. Is he waiting for me to ask? That wouldn't make much sense.

I sneak a glance toward my captor and caretaker. He doesn't notice me watching, too concentrated on the dried herbs laid out in front of him. This is a usual occurrence, when he is busy with ointments and medicines that he readies for the next ailing villager. I have nothing to do but watch him break them apart, mix them in the mortar, and place different concoctions in tiny, clay vessels.

It's soothing to watch, and rather fascinating, but I'd never tell Stillwater that.

Today, he bends over his task, raven hair falling across his face because he never binds it. Every so often, his gaze will slide in my direction, brows still furrowed in concentration, and I quickly look away.

Perhaps I have just grown too bored, holed up in this tepee with no windows to look out, just that tiny, little hole in the top. There are so many bundles of drying herbs hanging around that my nose tickles, and I get so excited when the flap opens and I can get a brief glimpse outside. It seems silly, I know... just about as silly as me thinking that Stillwater is quite handsome. He would make a good husband. I guess when you stare at someone for so long, it can have that effect.

My cheeks flush. Where did that even come from, and when did I start thinking about that kind of thing? I want to smack myself for even pondering it. Even if Stillwater is kind and understanding toward me, he is still an Indian. What my Pa and everyone else who had a mind called wild and untamed. His kindness toward me is getting to my head, and I can't let it because I know what happens when you find someone attractive. You think you've fallen in love, and that's the one thing I promised myself against, because it always leads to heartbreak, and in my hometown, there's no such thing as romance and love. If a man wants a woman, then he will ask her parents or the nearest relative for her. A woman didn't get to pick who she married, no matter how much she wished for it. Her life-mate was simply chosen, and that was that. Just how it would have been with Adam Saunders.

I sigh for the second time in an hour.

"Why do you stare?" Stillwater breaks my tortured thoughts, and I jump.

His hands stop turning and grinding, his eyes gazing at me for my answer. An answer I refuse to give. I can't tell him I find him 'kind to the eyes'. I would rather turn into a puddle on the ground.

Before they betray me, I turn my eyes away from him. "I was thinking about how much I would like to get some fresh air and see something besides this tepee," I say before I clam up. After all, I really want to go outside more than anything right now. The worst thing he can do is refuse me.

Stillwater hums in thought. "The sun is setting. Would you like to watch it go down?" He sets his things to the side and stands up.

I haven't even answered yet, but he takes my hand and helps me to my unsteady feet. I sway at first, and he grabs me to keep me from teetering backward.

"Does your leg hurt?" Stillwater inquires, and I shake my head. Slowly, he releases all but my hand and leads me to 'freedom,' or the closest thing to it.

The moment we step outside, I forget to breathe. The sun sets low over the horizon and casts a purple glaze over the group of tepees facing toward the east. A few people mull about, preparing things to be ready for the new day. They look toward us and continue on their merry way. I'm a little surprised that no one looks at me funny.

Almost as if reading my thoughts, Stillwater guides me toward a log sitting in front of a smoldering fire. "No one will bother you." Those words are not what I was told to believe but a few days ago. If that were the case, then why hasn't he allowed me to walk around the village on my own?

We sit down, side by side, in silence for a while, watching the camp prepare for sleep.

"My father's sister, White Deer, is going to take you in tomorrow. She will teach you our ways." His words seem loud in the quiet twilight. Or is it because of what he's saying about me moving? Of course, I knew staying in his tepee was temporary as his patient. I can't stay there anymore. It would look bad, but I'm still nervous. I only hope his aunt is as nice as he is and not the one who despises my guts.

"H-How long am I staying here?" I don't specify if I mean with him or in this village. We haven't spoken of what's becoming of me. Not yet.

"You can stay here as long as you need. My father will allow it, even if the others disagree."

His father... I feel his father is a powerful man among their people, and that's a little unsettling.

"What if I want to be with my people? I could try to find my family." I watch Stillwater look down, contemplating my words.

"I can take you to the white man's fort before the snows come, if that is what you wish."

I don't know what I wish for my future, if there even is a future. It seems so bleak right now, not having anywhere I belong.

"What I wish for right now is to see my grandmama's grave and make sure all is well." I dare try to ask for what's been bothering me for a while. I need to know that the wolves haven't destroyed her resting place. Then I can try to close that part of my life. I just need a little closure, and then I will never wish for my old life again. That part of my life will be over. I should decide where I belong. Maybe this woman called White Deer can help me figure this out.

That night, I go to sleep like all the other nights before.

THE WAY OF THINGS

I stand in a clearing. Howls fill the air, and I tell myself not to look behind me. I run. Toward the forest. Toward the figure standing just at the edge. Stillwater. At first, I'm not sure he's even there, but then he takes a step toward me.

Wolves surround me, but I have to get away. I have to get to Stillwater. I aim a pistol at the wolf closest to me, and the shaggy beast drops to the ground. The other two beside it stop digging to stare at me, and I step back. I shouldn't have done that. Not again.

I whip around in terror at the sound of a growl behind me, but there's no time to react. No time to lift the gun again and shoot. I hit the ground on my back, and gray fur blurs in front of me.

The wolf that stalked me from behind pins me to the dirt. I recoil from the familiar scent of its foul breath as its sharp fangs inch closer to my face. My hand still grips the pistol, and I point it up, cock it, and pull the trigger. It gives a funny, little click, and my stomach drops in horror.

The gun is empty again...

I tremble as drool drips from the animal's jowls, and he snarls as if he knows he has me now. The other wolves gather closer as if to watch us.

I don't know if I'll survive it this time, but I refuse to die lying down. Once again, I slam the pistol into the wolf's face, and he yelps and jolts away from me. In the split second I'm free, I don't dare waste any time. I roll away and am on my feet, running toward Stillwater. But he's not alone. A wolf is creeping up behind him, ready to strike. I scream for him to watch out before something slams me to the ground face first.

"HOLLY?" SOMETHING SOFT brushes my cheek, and my eyes snap open wide. Stillwater sits beside me.. He looks worried.

"Stillwater?" I say quietly, but it comes out in a croak. I shiver from the horror of the dream. It was worse this time. I look up at him.

"You were restless and mumbling in your sleep. I just wanted to make sure you were all right."

"It was just a dream," I assure him, but I can't quell the tremors running through me. A nightmare is a much better word.

"You've had these often." Stillwater brushes the hair from my face, and my traitorous, little heart skips. I should be glad I'm not staying here anymore. If I don't leave soon, I think I'll lose myself.

"It was about the wolves." I try to calm the shaking, but my body won't listen.

Frowning, Stillwater pulls me closer until I nestle my head into the crook of his neck. "They can't reach you here."

I nod, breathing in deeply. Sweet pine... how pleasant.

The shivers fade at this distraction even as I blanch at my own thoughts. "I worry that they've dug up my grandmama's grave." I pull away and settle back on the furs, and now try to calm my breathing. "I had a horse, but he escaped that night, and I'm quite sure the wolves got to him."

"We can visit the cabin after the sun rises." Stillwater pats my head and shifts away to stand on his feet.

"Wait!" What am I doing? I grab his hand to pull him back. He turns back to me in surprise. "Could you wait for me to fall asleep?"

Stillwater smiles. It's the most beautiful thing I've seen, and I want to kick myself for thinking such things.

Stillwater

In only a matter of minutes, Holly is asleep, and I'm free to go back to my side of the tepee, but I don't. Instead, I sit for a few moments and watch over her. It's been only seven moons since she's come here, but I feel such a strong endearment towards her. I'm not sure if this is a good thing or bad. I've become more concerned over her well-being and whether or not she's happy. I worry when she's not, and fret about her situation. What has come over me? I've never felt this way before, and it's unsettling, and more than likely dangerous. I tell myself it's simply because she's alone and needs a friend. Yes, that's it. It wouldn't be a good idea to get attached to someone who likely will be gone soon. Holly doesn't belong here in this village and wild land. My people will never treat her as one of our own, and if they did, it would take a long time. Our lives are too different.

Chapter 6

Holly

My steps are shaky but sure as I keep pace behind Stillwater. The path leading to the cabin is unfamiliar, and I don't know where we are until we enter the woods where I had gathered the willow bark.

Stillwater slows his steps, looking behind him to make sure I'm still there. I'm aware I'm walking very slowly, but my legs just won't... go. But I'm determined to get back to the homestead to make sure Grandmama's grave is still intact, and if it isn't, then I'm also determined to set it right.

My captor and savior hasn't mentioned me ever coming back here to stay, and I'm almost relieved that I'm not destined to live here alone. I would be lying, though, if I said I'm not nervous about going to live in his aunt's tepee. I can't keep staying with Stillwater because, just like anywhere else, people would talk. If I stay much longer with his people, he said I would need to be married or adopted into a family. I want neither, but what am I to do?

"We are here." Stillwater stops right in front of me. I ram into his back then spring away to rub my smarting nose. He pretends he doesn't notice, and I pretend it never happened. I keep a safe distance this time, stepping toward the mound of piled stones.

They are mostly all there. One side has caved in, but thankfully, the body is still buried as it should be, though the grave is extremely shallow.

I let out a relieved sigh and sit on the ground. A shadow falls over me, but I don't look up. Stillwater is quiet and lets me sit in silence. After a while, he squats down beside me and begins placing the stones back into place. I turn to look at him, but his eyes are closed, and I wonder if he's praying. It seems odd since he never knew the woman who lies here, but nonetheless, I am touched. Once again, he throws me and my feelings for a loop. I still don't know what to make of this caring person. He just doesn't fit Pa's description of the heathens that live out west.

My betrothed is more heathen than this man.

Stillwater places the last stone and then turns to me. "She will be at peace now."

I nod, moisture pooling in my eyes, and I try hard not to spill any more tears.

"You cannot come back here again. It's not safe enough," Stillwater says as he stands up. He's not demanding that I never come back. He just thinks it's not safe because of the wolves.

I don't argue and rise to my feet to follow him. He makes his way back toward the woods, and we continue in silence, looking for Dusty, who ran in this direction. To my dismay, we find evidence of a big carcass a few yards to the left of the cabin as we pass. The poor animal.

I can't help but feel like I'm closing a chapter in my life, and it feels bittersweet. Farewell, Grandmama.

I no longer belong in the life I lived, and now I'm not sure where I belong. Certainly not at the fort, and definitely not with Stillwater and his people. If only I could get on another ship and sail to that land of rolling green hills, but alas, I cannot. All I can do now is face forward.

Stillwater's aunt, White Deer, is not at all who I imagined. I imagined a wizened, old woman, but in actuality, she is no more than forty years of age. Old enough to be wise, but young enough to be lively and energetic. She reminds me of a younger version of Grandmama, and I feel a painful pang in my chest, though I can't help but smile. I start to believe that I might make it in this village, at least until I can go to the fort and try to catch another wagon train by the next spring.

Stillwater converses with White Deer, and she nods to him and looks at me with a smile. There's no malice in her expression, and she looks more curious about me than anything else. Lifting her hand, the woman picks up a lock of my hair and studies it with wonder. She mutters something, and I look at Stillwater for a translation.

He grins at me. "White Deer says your hair is the color of fire."

"Oh." I smile at White Deer. "Thank you."

She nods at me.

"Do not let her fool you. She knows more white words than you think," Stillwater says quietly, but loudly enough for his aunt to hear.

White Deer narrows her eyes at him playfully and makes a shoo-ing motion, saying something in Lakota.

"She wants me to leave because she wishes to scrub and dress you." He pats me on the shoulder. "I will see you later, little dove." Then he leaves me alone before I can say a word. With her. White Deer. The woman circles me, taking measurements with her eyes. Nodding, she hums to herself and leaves me standing to rummage in the corner of her lodging. She returns with a beautiful, deerskin dress and holds it out to me. "You," she says.

I take it gingerly. "Th-Thank you."

"Now. Follow." She passes through the tepee doorway.

I stumble after Stillwater's aunt. She's talking in her mother tongue so fast that, even if I knew the language, I couldn't keep up. We pass the tepees and head toward a creek fifteen to twenty paces away. I trot after, and we stop in front of the rippling water. She points at a deeper section of the creek. "You. Bathe."

My eyes widen, and I turn to look back at the village. A few bushes obscure the view of the creek. Just enough to hide someone, but not enough to suit me. "No. I don't need a bath." I shake my head at her, hoping that she understands.

White Deer points at the water. "You. Go." She places the fresh dress on a rock.

I know she's right. I haven't had a proper bath in a while. Especially since being on the wagon train. I clamp my mouth closed and remove the soiled, white dress full of dirt and old blood. Throwing it to the ground, I take my first step into the water with a gasp and quickly leap back onto the bank. It's too cold.

"No. No." White Deer shakes her head. "Go." She steps closer to the edge of the bank, forcing me back into the creek. "Wash."

I step back into the icy water, gritting my teeth to keep them from chattering. Knowing that she won't let me out of the water until I do, I start scrubbing my skin and hair of the grime they accumulated. I don't have any soap, but it works just the same.

Finally, I'm clean from head to toe and trembling with cold. White Deer takes a step to the side to let me back onto the bank.

Once I'm dry enough to get dressed, we walk back to the tepees, and I take a moment to focus on what I'm wearing. Delicate beads run across the bodice, and the fringe tickles my forearms as they swing while I walk. I'm wearing a work of art. Nothing I've ever owned has been as beautiful as this dress.

I glance toward my caretaker in gratitude. Realizing that I've been a little less than grateful for that cold wake up call, I take her hand, and she stops to stare back at me in surprise. "Thank you, White Deer." I give her a smile.

"You are welcome." She smiles back.

Outside White Deer's tepee, Stillwater is talking to a giant of a man. My steps falter, and they both turn to stare at me. Stillwater blinks. The hulking giant nods to me and breaks eye contact just as quickly, as if he doesn't know where to look. For someone so big, he seems very shy.

"This is Tall Bear. He is a friend." Stillwater gestures toward the man.

A tiny smirk tries to take over my face, and I can't help but laugh because the name is so very fitting. "Nice to meet you, Tall Bear." I stretch out my hand, and he looks at it then back at me in puzzlement.

"He does not understand very many words in the white man's tongue. He believes it is a waste of time," Stillwater explains to me. "Don't let him scare you."

I drop my hand, feeling foolish. It seems no one shakes hands around here in greeting. I clear my throat and do the only thing anyone could in my situation. I smile.

Tall Bear smiles back.

White Deer guides me into the tepee, gesturing for me to sit down on the furs. I sit without complaint and try not to shiver from the cold. I'm still a little chilly from my adventure in the creek. The men don't follow us and, instead, stay outside.

THE WAY OF THINGS

White Deer sits behind me and combs through my hair, gently removing tangles. I'm aware of something stinky she runs through my tresses. My nose curls of its own accord, but I don't say a word and sit straight. I admire the woman's ability to tame my wild, red curls into one loose plait going over my shoulder. With her handy work done, White Deer nods. "Good." She gives me a smile and stands up. "Stay. I go get food."

"Thank you," I say again.

After White Deer hands me a bowl of what looks like venison, I eat quietly while she fixes up my 'corner' of the tepee. Should I really call it a corner? It's an infinite circle, after all. When I think about it, it's a bit funny. I'm not used to being in a tepee just yet. Especially when you can see the sky through the tiny, little peephole. It hasn't rained yet, and I wonder if rain goes straight down through it.

After she makes sure I'm well fed, she steps outside to call Stillwater. He comes through without his friend this time. White Deer smiles at him and pats his cheek.

He turns his brown eyes to me. "I have someone important for you to meet. Do you feel well enough to walk a little more this day?" Stillwater stretches his hand out to me, and I take it. He hauls me to my feet, and I sway for a moment. I'm not quite recovered just yet, and if I'm to be honest, I'd much rather lie down and go to sleep, but I wouldn't refuse Stillwater after all he's done for me.

So, I step outside with him, aware that he has a hold of my hand and hasn't let go of it. Strangely, I don't mind and follow him.

An older man calls to Stillwater from a few tepees away, and my feet glue to the ground. He's wearing a headdress and looks quite important. I pin him immediately as the chief named Strong Wind that White Deer mentioned in passing. Stillwater waves at him and says the one word I know is father. I feel my mouth fall straight open. Stillwater is the chief's son?

I follow slowly behind Stillwater as he approaches the chief, then I stand directly behind him because, let's face it, facing an actual chief is a little scary. He's the one that has the say whether I stay or go.

They exchange a few words, and I just know that they're talking about me, but I refuse to step into view until Stillwater reaches behind himself and grabs a hold of my wrist.

I give a squeak of protest as I'm hauled to his side once more. I stare up at the chief—Stillwater's father. There is no resemblance at all, but I try not to stare. Chief Strong Wind nods at me with a pleasant expression. "Hello," he says in accented English.

"Hello," I say back quietly.

"Stillwater has told me many things about you."

I look up at Stillwater. His ruddy cheeks turn even more red, and he looks away from us as if embarrassed.

"I hope good things." A nervous titter comes out of me.

"Never bad." He nods to his son. "We welcome you to our village. You may stay as long as you need to."

"Th-Thank you, sir." I smile.

Chapter 7

Holly

D ays pass by, one by one, and I slowly fall into a routine with White Deer, who shows me all the tasks the women of the village do every day.

How to build a proper fire and even how to weave a basket. Not that I'm any good at the weaving bit. No one can say I didn't try, of course. It just looked less like a basket and more like a porcupine, and made everyone have a good laugh. Stillwater works with me an hour or two a day to learn the language, and I'm happy to say I string along quite a few words. It's much easier to talk to White Deer now. Everyone was a little wary of me at first, but Chief Strong Wind made sure that no one bothered me. They decided I was more curious-looking than a threat to them. Having Stillwater at my side helped since he's the chief's son. I'm still quite shell shocked, but it makes sense now how Stillwater can drag me to his village and everyone just lets him.

I follow Stillwater on his foraging days, helping him gather herbs for himself and Healing River, who has grown too old to do it. I love learning about the different plants and flowers I never even knew existed. The main staple among all medicines, of course, is willow bark, the red-wooded species of which is referred to as

Cansasa by the Lakota and gathered up almost daily. I help him grind the herbs, but some we simply hang to dry. His work is almost never done, and with everything White Deer has me do and all of my free time spent around Stillwater, my days are full, and I barely have time to ponder my circumstances. If I'm a captive in this village, I don't feel like one. More like I just belong here.

I can't deny that I love my simple, new life, and White Deer is so much like Grandmama, it hurts. Now that I can somewhat understand the Lakota's words, we talk often and enjoy each other's company. I think the woman has adopted me as her own, though she's never said it outright. White Deer married quite young but lost her husband to the smallpox. She had no children. The closest thing she ever had to it was Stillwater, who seems to never stay away for long. It seems he enjoys my company just as much as I enjoy his. The help I give him in gathering medicine is much appreciated.

I confess our easy-won friendship has been slipping into something very strange. Every time he walks by, my heart does this little stutter, and my eyes refuse to focus on anything but him. And it seems I have the same effect on him, if the way he looks at me so often is any sign. This whole thing just makes me nervous because I'm not sure what it means. Surely, I can't be developing an attachment to him. I admit, I find him handsome, but he's not the only attractive man in the village, even if he is the only attractive man that has given me his company. I can't forget, I'm still betrothed to a man I don't want to marry.

Two Months Later

Stillwater

There is talk among the warriors of a group of dog soldiers terrorizing the wagon trains that have been passing through. I fear that is what happened to Holly's family. I have heard a few rumors of an attack with no survivors, except for one. A woman with hair the color of corn that matches the description of Holly's sister. I pray it is not so, but I fear the worst. I'm not even sure how to break this news to Holly. Is there a way to tell someone that their family has been massacred?

The longer I go without telling her, the sicker in my stomach I feel. I need to tell her before she hears word of it from someone else.

My thoughts are so consumed with what to tell her and when to tell her, I almost walk straight into a bramble.

"Watch out!" Small hands grab my forearm to hold me back from my prickly descent, and I jerk to a stop not a moment too soon.

Holly stands beside me, her small pile of willow bark shavings abandoned on the ground.

I shake my head at my carelessness and step around the bush to get to my destination. A patch of echinacea flowers. I can feel

Holly's worried gaze on me, but I try to ignore it. I don't know what to say if she asks me why I'm so distracted.

Holly has been a wonderful addition to the village. There are some who dislike the idea of her and stay away, but more than half of the villagers have welcomed her and try to help her to learn our ways. It's as if she's become a part of the village, even though she's not been formally adopted in. White Deer has unofficially adopted her as the daughter she never had. I can hardly imagine life without Holly in it. The idea of her going away makes me anxious, so I try not to think of it. But I know that eventually, I will have to.

I pluck the purple flowers and place them in the pouch attached to my belt.

We are far enough away from the village to not see the tips of the tepees, but close enough to hear people going about their day. That's how I first hear the approach of new horses.

I freeze and turn toward the sound.

"What's wrong?" Holly asks. Her words are too loud, and I inwardly cringe.

"Sssh." I make a shushing motion with my fingers.

Her eyes widen, and she stills beside me.

White men hardly ever venture into our territory, but that doesn't mean that they won't. This thought has me worried.

"We need to go back. Stay behind me," I whisper and start back the way we came.

Holly follows suit, stuffing her findings in her own pouch dangling from the belt around her doeskin dress.

Holly

Stillwater's behavior makes me nervous. Now that we're getting closer, I can hear unfamiliar voices and horses making a commotion. I stiffen, noticing how tense Stillwater has become. Something's not right.

We tiptoe on silent feet. Stillwater stirs not a leaf, and I'm aware of how many times my moccasins crunch over leaves and twigs, but he doesn't rebuke me. I don't believe I've ever seen him angry with me before. I am trying to be quiet. Too bad he hasn't taught me how to be stealthy just yet. I'm sure he wishes he had.

Pausing right outside the tepees, we peek behind one and focus on the newcomers. I gasp, forgetting myself, and step forward. Stillwater yanks me back.

I can see Chief Strong Wind and White Deer standing with most of the village staring ahead, but they don't see what I see.

"May?" Am I seeing things? A blonde woman stumbles into the village, led by a warrior on a horse. She's tied like a pack mule. There are several other warriors, but they don't have a captive, just oxen and horses. Some of these animals look familiar, and I get an unsettled feeling.

"Holly, go back inside," Stillwater insists, but I barely hear him, being so transfixed by the sight of the newcomers. My sister... Why is she here, and why is she not with the wagon train?

My legs threaten to keep me grounded, because seeing her can only mean one thing. I gasp and spin to face my captor. My only friend. "Did you know about this?" The silence that meets me is enough, but I wait for his answer, willing it not to be so.

"I learned a while ago that another band attacked the wagon train you were in." The horrified look on his face is genuine, but I'm struck that he never thought to tell me. How could he keep such things from me? I gave him my trust, and he betrayed me!

The man leading my sister is getting closer, and at this range, I can see the dirt and grime that covers her too-thin frame. The hollowness of her face and the scrapes and the blood all over her. Her eyes find me and hold fast. They narrow, and she mouths one word.

"No. It can't be." My ears buzz, and my words seem a faraway mumble. "Why is she here and not on her way to Oregon?"

"Holly, I'm sorry I didn't tell you that your wagon train was ambushed. It wasn't our people," Stillwater is saying, but his words are fuzzy, and I can't hear them over the roaring of my heart.

"No. It can't be. Tell me it's not so!" I shake my head in horror, but that's a mistake, and it makes my head swim. My vision tunnels, turning my world unexpectedly black.

Stillwater

One moment, Holly stands beside me, angry, and then the next, she collapses. I barely have time to grab her before she hits the ground. I cradle her against me and watch the strange dog soldiers stop at the entrance of our village. Some of our warriors greet them, happy to make a few trades. The girl is part of them, and I feel anxious. If I don't take her off the men's hands, they'll leave with her, and Holly might never see her again. Holly deserves this much, to keep her sister, and from the looks of the poor girl, she has been through something horrible.

Holly's sister continues to stare at her and then at me, and the look she gives me is of pure hatred. I shiver the moment our eyes meet.

"Let me take her," White Deer says, reaching for Holly. I lean her against a tree, and my aunt sits beside her.

"That captive is her sister. I must get her back," I say, torn between wanting to stay to make sure Holly is all right and getting her sister for her. White Deer shoos me away, and my decision is made. I walk toward the group.

"I know of Hooked Nose. He's notorious for his ruthless ways. I'll trade for the girl. No one deserves to be owned by a snake." Tall Bear steps in beside me. "You have enough on your hands with the fire-haired woman." We step toward the gathered party.

"You don't know what you're getting into." I shake my head at him, flabbergasted.

"I have no wish to keep a captive. Let her stay with her sister."

I watch my best friend go to the man with Holly's sister and bargain for her. I'm thankful to have a friend like him.

Holly's sister stares at Tall Bear, shrinking into herself. She looks like a frightened rabbit, cornered by two coyotes.

The dog soldier laughs, looking pleased at whatever trade Tall Bear is making, and before long, her former captor cuts her ropes and shoves her towards her new one. The girl stares up at him, scared out of her wits, and flinches the moment he reaches for his knife. Tall Bear pulls her wrists toward him. Cutting her bindings, he sends a scathing look toward Hooked Nose.

"You're a fool to let her go. She will kill you in your sleep. She's made of fire, that one." Hooked Nose shakes his finger at Tall Bear. "Teach her who she belongs to." It's my turn to glare at him.

Tall Bear turns the girl away from him and presses his hand on her back to guide her onward. She can't help but turn back to look at Hooked Nose.

The women in the camp are curious and reach to touch the girl's sun beam hair. Holly's sister hunches in on herself and keeps marching ahead. Her steps stutter at the sight of Holly, who is still unconscious beside White Deer. Once more, her gaze finds mine, and she glares.

"Holly!" she cries out, wrenching away from Tall Bear and the reaching hands. She runs to Holly's side and falls to her knees. White Deer watches the girl fret over her sister and looks back at me.

I'm taken aback by the moment the girl whirls around to face me. Anger clouds her blue eyes. "What have you done to my sister, you savage?!" She flings her fists at me, but Tall Bear is faster and yanks her back.

She ducks, as if expecting a blow, and Tall Bear and I meet eyes. Whatever happened to this girl must have been very disturbing for her to act in such a way.

White Deer bites her lip at the exchange.

"Please take both of the women inside, sister," says Father.

White Deer approaches the wild girl cautiously. "Please come." As soon as Tall Bear lets go of her, she bolts forward, tucking her arms into herself.

At first, I think she'll refuse, but I'm sure she knows that dealing with one Indian woman is better than two Indian men. With one scathing glance at Tall Bear and I, she trots after White Deer.

I follow behind them with Holly, leaving Tall Bear watching awkwardly behind us. He stays rooted beside the chief.

White Deer will have to work a miracle to get this girl put back together.

Chapter 8

Holly

The first thing I see when I open my eyes is the tiny peephole in the top of White Deer's tepee, and I feel more than see someone sitting beside me. I don't remember coming back here. When did I—?

I gasp and sit straight up, my eyes darting to the figure beside me. Her blonde hair is plaited on each side of her head, and her skin is clean from blood and dirt, but her blue eyes are hollow, and her face set in harsh lines. May meets my eyes but doesn't look all that happy to see me. Actually, quite the opposite, in fact.

"You're finally awake." Her words are flat; lifeless.

"May, how did you end up here? What about Ma and Pa?" I'm wide awake now.

May looks away from me, her face turning pale. "No one has told you?"

"Told me?" I suddenly feel sick, and I know what she's going to say next. I want to stop her, and yet I must hear what she has to say. I shake my head and grab her hand. "May, what happened?"

She turns her face back to mine, tears pooling in her eyes. "They're all dead, Holly. Murdered. Scalped."

"Wh-What?" I croak out. Stillwater had warned me already, but her words still buzz in my eyes as if I'm under water... drowning. I need air.

"These heathens that you have been living with. Their kind are the ones that attacked the wagon train. I didn't witness everyone who was killed, but I watched Ma and Pa, Holly. They were one of the first to go." She snatches her hand away from mine as if I'd burned her, tucking it away to hide its visible trembling. Her eyes turn glassy.

"No, May. Say it's not true." Sorrow clogs my throat, and fat, ugly tears roll down my face.

"They killed Ma and Pa and spared me. I ask myself every day why they didn't scalp me too. It would have been better that way. These people are animals, Holly. I have been starved and man-handled for months. I'm shocked I've even been brought here and treated this well."

"They're not so bad here," I try to insist, but I have no fight left inside me to argue more and my shoulders slump.

"You shouldn't let yourself become so close to them." May fixes me with a knowing glare. I stare back at her. Perhaps I should feel ashamed for letting myself become so close to Stillwater and his family, but I cannot. There are bad Indians and there are bad whites, just as there are good Indians and good whites. While I'm upset about May's horrible experience and the deaths of the people on the wagon train, I can't be mad at Stillwater for something he didn't do, and I wouldn't hold it against his people. Only the people that committed such horrid acts.

Strangely, I'm not as devastated as I thought I would be, hearing of my parents' deaths. They never treated me as their true daughter like they did May, though I am in grief for them. I'm devastated that May has been treated so horribly. She may not be my true blooded sister, but she is still my sister and the only family I have left.

"Stillwater is nothing like the men who took you."

"How can you prove that? How do you know he's not just trying to gain your trust and planning something dastardly?" May scoffs at me, and her words chafe me the wrong way.

"Grandmama died of a fever, and I was forced to bury her in a shallow grave. That night, wolves came and tried to dig it up. I went out to scare them off, but things didn't go as planned and the wolves tried to attack me. Stillwater saved me and brought me back here. I had caught Grandmama's fever, and he nursed me back to health. If he hadn't saved me and let me stay here, I would have died." I can tell my words haven't fazed her in the least.

"That man has bewitched you, Holly. You need to snap out of it. That handsome face will be your death." May doesn't sound so lifeless now. She raises her voice higher and higher, and her hand goes up. I flinch.

A breeze rushes past, and a strong hand grabs May's to keep her from striking me. It's Stillwater. Somehow, we both missed him coming inside. He refuses to look in my direction but looks toward May coolly. "No matter how angry you are, never raise your hand against a defenseless person, or you are as bad as those warriors that took you."

May gasps and wrenches her hand away. "You speak English."

Stillwater doesn't answer and turns away from the both of us. "I will be gone after the sun rises. Don't look for me." He leaves without another glance.

Stillwater

I turn away from the two sisters and keep myself from looking at Holly. If either knew my little secret, what would they have to say then?

The pale-haired woman is so full of hate in her heart that she was ready to strike her own sister. I don't like the idea of Holly staying with someone so unstable, but it isn't my place to tell her or White Deer so.

"That girl is going to need a lot of healing," White Deer says. I turn to look at her standing a few feet away from the tepee. By the look on her face, she's heard everything as well.

"I'm sorry she's become your burden to bear." My shoulders slump, and suddenly, I'm so tired. So tired of every bad thing that has happened and will happen.

"Don't you worry about me, dear boy." White Deer pats my face in her motherly way. She's the closest thing to a mother I have left, and I hope she might be able to warm May's frigid heart. She's been such a wonder to Holly.

"I will be away after the sun rises."

"Does Strong Wind know you're leaving?" White Deer prickles my conscience, and I flinch.

"He told me that Holly could stay until she was well again, and then we would talk about what was to be done." I glance toward the too quiet tepee and frown. "Holly had mentioned going to the

67

white man's fort when she first came here. Since her sister has come to stay, I think it's only right. I'll go tomorrow and make plans for them."

White Deer tuts. "Have you asked the girl what she wants? What she wants and what you think she needs might be two different things. Being hasty is not wise. Especially when matters of the heart are involved." She turns my chin toward her and grips it tighter than necessary. "The grass on the other side is not always greener. You of all people should know this, for you belong in both worlds. Neither is perfect. You must choose carefully."

"She doesn't belong here. You know as well as I do she doesn't, and the village does not always treat her fairly. Holly should not have to put up with it for the rest of her life. She probably misses her old life." I sigh, and White Deer drops my chin, looking at me in exasperation.

"That girl has lost everything already. Has she told you before that she's adopted, just like you?"

I shake my head, but I should have figured. The two sisters look too different. "That changes nothing. My feelings don't matter."

"What about hers, Stillwater? Ask her what she wants. Don't push her away. Not yet," White Deer says quietly, leaving me to stand alone.

My heart hurts, but I know what I must do.

Holly

May steps outside the tepee and, for a moment, I think she's run off. That is, until she gives a scream that could curdle blood.

Despite my woozy head, I shoot up from the pile of furs and race outside to face whatever foe that May has found. What I find outside would almost be amusing if May's fear of Indians wasn't so severe.

Tall Bear stands outside our tepee, where I'm sure Stillwater asked him to be. May stands in front of him, locked in place. Frozen and unable to move.

"May?" I step closer to her.

"No, Holly! Keep away from him!" She steps back, and Tall Bear frowns at her antics. "He's the one who took me away from the Indians who kept me captive." She sounds conflicted when she says this, as if she's not sure if that's a good thing or not. I would say that means he saved her, but I'm sure she doesn't see going from one Indian to another as being saved.

"May, this is Tall Bear. He's a friend of Stillwater and is here to keep us safe. He won't hurt us."

May sneers at poor Tall Bear. "I doubt he is any friend of ours, even if he is a friend of your Indian. You can't trust any of these people, Holly."

My Indian? I sigh inwardly. My patience is going to be tested a lot today. I can already tell. Whatever happened to May during her time as a captive must have been a lot worse than she will ever tell us.

One day, I hope she will finally tell me. I want to understand where all her hatred is coming from. It can't only be because Indians killed our parents. It's so much more.

Tall Bear's eyes dart between us, and if I didn't know any better, I'd think he can understand every word we say.

White Deer appears, looking flustered. "Danger?" Her eyes are wide and frightened.

May jerks away from her when she reaches for her face.

I shake my head at White Deer. "We're fine."

Tall Bear furrows his brow and says something to White Deer. She laughs then, and he scowls. Whatever was said wasn't funny to him. She pats him on the back and releases him from guard duty.

White Deer gathers us and guides us back into the tepee. May stops and looks behind herself to stare at Tall Bear. Something flickers in her eyes, but it's not disgust. I think there might be hope for my sister and her hate-filled heart yet.

May is quiet the rest of the day, watching White Deer and I prepare for supper. She does attempt to help me gather firewood but ends up dropping most of the sticks. Her body is weak from being malnourished and beaten.

I worry about her internal injuries. She's a hollow shell of a girl and never speaks unless spoken to first or otherwise angered, as I've found out. She simply sits and watches with her eyes, moving about like a puppet when asked to do something.

She's wary of men, especially Tall Bear. She's relaxed only slightly since Stillwater left. May likes him less than Tall Bear, and I

70

know it's because of his interest in me. My sister has warmed up to White Deer. It seems her hate extends toward the males rather than females. I'm beginning to wonder what had become of her during her months as a captive. I'm suspecting that Hooked Nose did more than just beat her. My stomach sours at the thought. I'm more than sure that he touched her, and I can't ask her about it because she clams up every time I mention the time we were separated. I can only wait and hope she soon feels comfortable enough to tell me what happened. I feel like I'll be waiting for a very long time.

Days pass, and there's no sign of Stillwater. I become anxious. He didn't even tell me where he was going. Only that he was going away and leaving Tall Bear in charge of looking over us in his stead. I miss him more than I probably should. I'm growing rather fond of the man. One day, I'll leave this place, and I'll never see him or White Deer and the others again. The life I've made here will be for naught. I've tried to distance myself, to not grow so many attachments, but it was too late to stop it.

Tall Bear makes good on his word to Stillwater and sticks around during the day to keep watch over us. Not to get the wrong idea that he's making sure we 'sisters' don't run away. Not at all, but I think May perceives it as so. The Lakota are protective of the women in the tribe. Maybe more so than a white community. Everyone is treated with great respect... even as an outsider of the tribe. If I wasn't going away, I'm sure they would have adopted me in. White Deer has made it known that I'm like a daughter to her.

IT'S DAY THREE OF STILLWATER'S absence that May and I sit under a big oak tree where I clumsily attempt to make another basket. May watches intently beside me, brow furrowing at the mess I'm making.

"Can I try?" she says, sounding eager for the first time since we've been reunited. She reaches toward my porcupine basket, and I grudgingly surrender it over. With great interest, she turns it around, staring at my work so far. Without another word, she slowly turns the mess into a beautiful piece of art. She was always the crafty one in the family, always able to make a dress out of scrap material that most people would throw away. I was better outside... in the dirt.

I watch in fascination at how little time she takes to figure out basket weaving.

Tall Bear sits a few trees away, whittling a piece of wood with a knife. Every so often, he looks up to watch us—to watch May. He would never say it to anyone, but I think he finds my sister fascinating, and I wonder if May notices how he watches her. He always wears a unique expression when it comes to her. A softening of his eyes.

In a little over an hour, May presents me with my—her—finished basket. It looks almost as perfect as White Deer's, and I'd be lying if I said I wasn't jealous. She's a natural.

Tall Bear stands up, holding something behind his back. He quietly steps toward us. May tenses up at first, watching him like prey would a predator. He stops in front of us and extends his hidden hand out toward her. She cringes for only a second, until her eyes widen in surprise.

A tiny bear rests in the palm of Tall Bear's hand. It's so perfect and realistic. May stares at it, bringing her eyes up to meet Tall Bear's.

"For me?" She asks in Lakota. I've tried to teach her a few words, even though she outright refused at first. She's learning quite a lot, and I'm proud of her for it.

Tall Bear nods, taking her hand and pressing the little bear into it. He closes her hand around it and smiles. It's not my imagination, watching my sister's cheeks turn a slight rose.

"Thank you, Tall Bear."

I turn away, trying not to smile. "I'm going to show White Deer your basket." I excuse myself, leaving the two alone.

On my way back to White Deer's tepee, I'm startled by pounding horse hooves. I stop to stare toward the noise, my pulse picking up in time with the beats, and I nearly drop the basket in my excitement. I set it outside the tepee and turn back toward the approaching horse.

"Stillwater!" I call, racing toward the big, black mare.

Heads turn to stare at my antics, but I'm much too happy to be ashamed of myself.

Stillwater slows to a stop and watches me with a shocked expression. I immediately try to tamp down my excitement. This isn't how a Lakota woman would act. Not like I'm a Lakota woman at all, but I think I've embarrassed him in front of the villagers by accident. Now I have everyone gawking at us, stopping all activity in the camp.

I slide to a stop in front of him, feeling foolish now that I'm here. Now I'm equally as embarrassed as he is. "Hello," I say quietly.

Stillwater shakes his head and chuckles. "I've never received such a welcome before."

"I've missed you." The words come out before I can stop them, and I want to bite my tongue.

"I've missed you too," he whispers so only I can hear. But even as he says it, I notice his eyes are sad, and I wonder why.

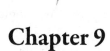

Chapter 9

Holly

Something is wrong with May. At first, it was so subtle I didn't notice, but now I can't help but notice. She barely eats a thing, and when she does, she runs out of the tepee so fast she nearly falls on her face. White Deer stares after her and just shakes her head. She knows something I don't. I can see it in her eyes. But May won't say a word, and neither will White Deer.

Today is no exception. As soon as May takes a bite of roasted fish, she jumps to her feet and runs out of the tepee, leaving White Deer and I in stunned silence. Stillwater, Tall Bear, and Chief Strong Wind sit on the opposite side of the fire, watching with a frown.

I make to get up to chase after her, but Tall Bear stands up instead and, in silence, steps out of the tepee, walking in the direction May went.

I stare in fascinated shock. Since when have those two gotten so close? I send a pointed look toward Stillwater, but he only furrows his brows.

It's all I can do to keep myself seated and not go investigating. I want to see what they're up to so badly, but I continue eating my fish in my silence. Conversation goes around, but I only nod when it's needed and appropriate. Many minutes later, May and Tall Bear come back to eat, or rather Tall Bear does. May sits back beside me, nursing a cup of water.

"Are you all right?" I lean toward May in question.

She looks at me in surprise. "Yes. Something didn't agree with me."

A lot of things don't agree with her lately, but I don't say it. You have to walk on eggshells around her these days. She panics over the littlest things.

"I went to the fort and spoke to the Colonel. They expect you in three moons." Stillwater's words steal my appetite, turning the fish in my mouth into ash. I haven't thought about leaving this place in a while. I've almost forgotten that I don't belong here; that I'm an outsider. I feel so at home in this village. More than I've ever felt anywhere except with Grandmama.

"That's wonderful news!" For the first time that I've ever seen, May smiles at Stillwater.

"Yes, wonderful news," I echo back, forcing a smile.

White Deer pats my hand. "You will be missed when you leave."

"I will miss this place," I say truthfully. A little voice inside begs to stay in this simple life. When have I ever enjoyed life more than I do now? Tears sting my eyes, and I blink them away.

"Excuse me." I turn away and dart out of the tepee before I make a fool out of myself. To cry is to show weakness, and no one needs to know my weakness.

I stop on the outskirts of the village camp, catching my breath. I need to get a hold of myself. This isn't how I should be. I should be happy that life is about to get back to normal. Whatever normal is. There's only one outcome for a lone woman in the middle of nowhere. Married to a stranger. The thought has me feeling cold. May isn't mentally stable and definitely isn't marriageable material. We would both be doomed to a miserable life out there. Can't Stillwater see this? Perhaps I'm being selfish. These people have been more than hospitable. It wouldn't be fair to expect to stay here.

My shoulders slump in defeat.

"Holly?" It's May. I turn to look at her, furiously wiping at my eyes before she sees my tears. She wouldn't understand why I would be sad to leave here. She can't wait to get away.

She walks toward me slowly. I almost feel bad that she felt she needed to find me.

"You should go back. You're unwell." I grab her hand and lead her to a log, and she sits down heavily.

"I'm fine. Only tired. I feel better than I did. Promise." She smiles at me, and I relax. She seems genuinely better. "Are you excited to finally go back to a white settlement?"

No.

"Yes, it will be nice to sleep in a real bed and take a bath in water that isn't as cold as ice." I laugh. This much is true, at least. I miss the little things like that. There are no people I wish to be with. None.

We sit quietly, both thinking of the upcoming time to leave for the fort. For once, May is the positive one.

The next day, I once again notice May accompanying Tall Bear. If he's not on a hunt with the other warriors or with Stillwater, he seems to be with my sister. I'm struck by how friendly they've become. Was it just a few weeks ago that she was scared to death of the man? Now she would rather be with him than anyone else at the camp. I wonder if she feels regret leaving this village as much as I and just pretends she can't wait to leave. She gets along so well with White Deer nowadays.

Letting curiosity get the better of me, I decide to follow May and Tall Bear closely behind. I've learned a thing or two about walking quietly... like an Indian. Many of the things I've learned while living in this village will be quite valuable to remember. I'll miss the freedom of doeskin and short skirts.

Tall Bear and May disappear past the tepees and keep walking into the woods. I dart from tree to tree, feeling frustrated. Where are they going?

They walk side by side in silence and then stop close to the creek. Tall Bear gestures toward a couple of boulders, and May sits down. Her face is tired, but she looks happy. In fact, much happier than I've ever seen her.

I squint. This is getting fishy. These would be the last two people in this village I'd expect to get all chummy.

Something touches my arm, and I open my mouth to scream. A hand quickly comes down on my mouth, and I'm shoved further behind the tree.

"Sssh!" Stillwater chastises.

I wrench his hand away and glare at him. "You scared me."

"You shouldn't listen in on others' conversations." Stillwater gives me a look.

"I just wanted to know what these two have been up to."

"That's their business and not yours." Stillwater shakes his head and leads me away. "I believe they have an understanding, and May enjoys talking to him because he doesn't talk back or understand her language."

I step on a twig and cringe when it snaps, but keep walking. "I don't believe Tall Bear doesn't understand English. He always looks like he's listening in."

"I tried to teach him many years ago, but he would have nothing to do with it. Perhaps he's learned some words on his own." Stillwater leads me back toward the tepees. "White Deer has been looking for you. She wants your help with scraping the hides."

I grimace. That's one of the hardest jobs I've endured, and it takes hours to scrape hair off stinky animal hides. "I will see you later, then." We stop further down the creek. He grabs my hand before I can leave.

"Wait."

I turn back to look at him in surprise. "Is something the matter?" All I can concentrate on is his hand holding onto mine.

"There's a full moon tonight... I... was wonderingifyou'dliketowatchittonight." Stillwater clears his throat.

"What?" Was that even English? It didn't sound like Lakota either.

Stillwater scowls at me playfully, as if it's a hard thing for him to say it all over again. "I was wondering if you'd like to watch the full moon tonight. It will be the last one you see here. It might be hard to watch the sky with so many walls at the fort." At the word fort, he seems to wilt, and I want to wilt with him.

"I would like that." I smile at him and then spin on my heels, leaving him standing there.

"There you are." White Deer hands me a bone scraper the second I walk up, and I take it begrudgingly.

"I went on a walk with Stillwater." I scrape down, gritting my teeth.

"I was wondering where you went. You didn't think I'd start without you." She smiles at me.

Scrape.

Scrape.

Scraaaaape.

"He asked me if I'd watch the full moon with him tonight."

White Deer chuckles. "You would make a fine wife for Stillwater. It is a shame you will be leaving."

I sputter. "Wife?" I hit a snag and scowl at it.

"A man who asks a woman on walks and moon viewing is looking for a wife," she says simply, as if I'm supposed to know these things.

My face burns.

"What's this about a wife? Is someone getting married?" a new voice says.

I nearly jump out of my skin and stare up at May, who's holding a big bowl of ashes and a container of water. My nose curls again. The nauseating smell is getting to me. Thankfully, all that is left is to remove the deer hair.

"No. No one is getting married around here," I say hurriedly.

"Good." May sets the bowl down, steering clear of the hides. "I will prepare the fire for meal preparations."

We finish scraping and soak the hides in ash water. I make a prompt escape after we stretch them out. My nose already burns with the idea of mushed deer brains that I've watched White Deer smear over the hides in an act of curing them. She assures me she can do that task when the time comes. Maybe it's a good thing I'm leaving this place. I can't stomach some things they do, but there's no denying that their buckskin is the best quality I've ever seen.

THE WAY OF THINGS

Done for now, we walk back to prepare supper. It's venison stew for the night since the warriors brought back so many deer today.

Chapter 10

Holly

"What has you so fretful?" May asks in annoyance.

I jump, dropping my hand from my hair, abandoning efforts of taming it into a neater braid. "Nothing. Just trying to fix my hair."

"I heard Stillwater invited you to watch the moon tonight. Sounds like he wants to court you, sister," May says with disapproval.

I laugh, and it's too loud. "Don't be so silly, May. He doesn't want to court me. He doesn't like me like that." Does he? "We're leaving. He wouldn't want to court me." I tear the tie out of my hair and fluff the braid out. My hair refuses to be tamed tonight. Oh well.

May sits down in front of me. "Please remember that Stillwater may be cultured and polite, but he is still one of them. A savage. Never forget that."

"He's not a savage, May." I cringe at her choice of words.

She scoffs, but I don't miss the grimace she makes, suddenly gripping her stomach as if it pains her.

"Are you all right? You look a little pale." I reach out to touch her forehead, and she jerks backward.

"I'm just tired." She scoots away and lays down on her furs. "I think I'll take a nap, if you don't mind." Her hand wraps around the wooden bear nestled atop the furs. She caresses the thing when she's worried.

I frown after her and look outside. Twilight is casting the ground in purples and shadows. I stand up. "I will let you sleep then."

She doesn't say another word, so I leave her be. We can talk later.

Stillwater stands by the large oak tree right outside the village, waiting for me. I sit down and prop my back against its wide trunk, and he joins me.

At first, we don't speak, and I wonder why he's called me out here.

"Are you looking forward to going to Fort Stellar?" Stillwater asks me innocently, unaware of the knife he jabs into my heart.

"Not really. I think May is much more excited." I can't lie to him. He'll see right through it.

The moon shines above us, big and bright. It's what 'my people' would call a harvest moon. The breeze blows through trees and through the tepees, tickling the hair around my face. I shiver and wish I'd brought the fur cape White Deer gifted me.

"You're cold," Stillwater says.

"Just a little, but I'm fine." I sound like my sister now. 'I'm fine.' Those are her favorite words.

Stillwater gives a sigh. "My people are having a gathering. A feast to celebrate the changing season."

I perk up and turn to him. "When?" I was told that their feasts were always something to look forward to. Music and dancing. I would have liked to see it.

"I won't get to be a part of it. It's on the night I take you to the fort." His eyes are sad, and I wonder if it's because he'll be missing the celebration or because he's sending me away.

"Oh. I was looking forward to it." I can't help my disappointed tone. It's more than just my body that's cold. My heart feels frozen, ready to burst into a million little shards. "Perhaps I do want to get my cape." I rise to my feet.

"Holly," my name rolls off his lips, and I close my eyes. He grabs my hand to keep me rooted. I should just go and not look back. Every moment I spend with him is another moment of feeling closer. Closer to getting my heart broken. In only a day, I will leave for the fort, and I will never see Stillwater again. Just the thought pulls hard at me and leaves me feeling raw. Why do I feel so hurt about going away? Just a few months ago, I couldn't wait to get away from this place, and now... just the thought of leaving this man makes me want to cry. I should check on May. She isn't feeling well.

"Please look at me."

Against my better judgment, I do.

Those brown eyes hold mine fast, and I'm pulled away from the reality of the cold, hard world, and it's only Stillwater and I.

"Stillwater?" His name is a whisper because I can't find my tongue. He holds onto my hand and doesn't let go. I see a glimpse of a sheen in his eyes, and then I'm pulled into his arms, and he rests his chin on top of my head, and I can no longer see him.

"You will be missed." His voice is strained, as if it's hard to speak. I try to look up at him, but he presses my head back down as if embarrassed by his emotions.

"I'm not gone yet," I protest, but my words die on my tongue as something wet hits my cheek. "Why can't I stay here with you and White Deer?"

"You don't belong here." His words slice through my heart, and I inwardly wince. Who is to decide my fate? Who gets the final decision of whether I belong or not? He just assumes that I don't want to stay here... stay with him. I blink back the wetness in my eyes. I can't let him see me cry.

"Who decides if I belong or not?" I whisper so quietly I'm sure he doesn't hear me. His hair tickles my nose, and once more, I try to pull away. This time he lets me go easily, and I step back.

"Would you be willing to stay here and lose everything?" Stillwater asks me, demanding my full attention. If I wanted to look away, I couldn't.

"I have nothing to lose." I touch his cheek, and he leans into it. "Nothing but you, and I don't know if I can bear it." My voice trembles, and I bite my lip to keep from crying. "Don't make me leave you." I shake my head, and the tears disobey me and slip down my face.

Stillwater steps closer and touches both of my cheeks, rubbing his fingers over them to remove the wetness. "I thought you wanted to go back. Please don't cry, my dove."

My Dove. He's only called me that once before. Otherwise, I'm only ever Holly. The pet name endears him to me only that much more. I can't help it then. The tears begin to slip down my cheeks anew. I don't want to go to the fort, not anymore. I want to stay with him more than anything. All this time I spent trying to keep my distance. To not feel something, to not become too attached. It was all for naught.

"You belong with your people, and I belong with mine," Stillwater says, trying to sound convincing but falling short. He doesn't believe it any more than I do.

I take another step back to turn toward White Deer's tepee, but he grabs my wrist and pulls. I gasp and fall back into him, staring up in shock.

"I am selfish, Holly. I can't help but wish for things that cannot be."

"I am also selfish." When will he understand I don't want to leave him? That it gives me physical pain just to think of such things?

We stand there, right in the middle of the village in a lock of wills, unable to pull our eyes away. This feeling I have... is this what love feels like? It's a terrible and wonderful thing. We shouldn't be standing here like this. Someone could be watching.

Stillwater leans forward, pulling me close, and tilts my chin up to claim my mouth instead of answering me. Suddenly, I can't remember what was so important that we were talking about. I close my eyes and kiss him back with all I'm worth, pouring out everything that I didn't say to him, but wanted to. My hands find their way into those raven locks, fingers threading into the silken strands.

Stillwater squeezes me tighter. "Holly, I love—"

"Please... don't say it." I shake my head. "Don't say such things if you're going to send me away. Let me stay here." I'm begging, though I promised myself I'd never stoop so low. My fingers tighten their hold.

An eternity passes, but in reality only a few seconds. He releases me, and I mourn the loss of him already. Why can't I stay in that safe embrace just a little while longer?

The look on his face is full of pain, and I know what he's going to say before he even says it.

"It will never work. You will regret it someday." Stillwater presses a finger to my lips to quiet me and shatters the rest of my heart. "I must bring you and your sister to the fort as promised." He lets go of my lips to place a chaste kiss upon my brow. Almost in farewell.

"No, Stillwater. I won't leave you!" I grab his hand this time to pull him back, but he just shakes his head.

"Then I will be forced to leave you." He turns away from me and disappears.

I'm left standing in shock. A movement to my right makes me freeze. Rising Sun is watching us. She smiles in a frightful way, as if saying she knows something I don't. Something not pleasant. She turns away, and that's when I notice my sister standing beside her, watching in horror.

"Holly!" She strides toward me, her blonde plaits swinging and defying her otherwise Indian attire. She stops in front of me.

"How dare you!"

"What?" I take a step back, looking behind me as I do. Rising Sun has already disappeared. I turn back. "What are—?"

May backhands me, and my head whips to the side with the force of it. "You let him kiss you. How dare you, you little—" She raises her hand again, and I duck, eyes stinging from the pain. My ears ring like a church bell.

"May, please! Stop this!" I grab her hand and yank it down before she swings at me again.

"How could you, Holly?" Tears form in her eyes. "His people slaughtered our family, and you're letting him touch you. He's brainwashed you! If we stayed here, you would have married him without a second thought, and you'd lose yourself." She screams at me then. "You will most definitely lose me. I will have no part of a sister like you."

Her hand drops from mine, and it's all I can do to keep standing on my own two feet. My sister has such hatred. These people have been more kind to her than she deserves, and she still thinks they're evil. She turns away from me and stalks back toward White Deer's tepee.

I fall to my knees. Not because I am upset with myself for letting myself be kissed by 'the enemy,' but because my sister's heart is so full of hurt and anger, there is no room for love. She could hate everyone, but it wouldn't bring Ma and Pa back.

"Holly?!" Stillwater calls out. A shadow falls over my slumped form. A hand touches my back in worry, but I cannot speak. I'm crying too hard to say even two words. Right there in the open, Stillwater sits on his knees and pulls me close. I spill the rest of my bitter tears into his shoulder. "My sister is so angry, Stillwater."

"She has been through so much. It's only natural," Stillwater says into my hair. "It will take time for her to trust again."

"I don't think she will ever trust anyone here. She hates—" I begin to say and break off the words. I shouldn't tell him how much she despises him and his people.

"One day she will," Stillwater promises, as if he can see the future. Of course, it won't matter in the future because we're leaving.

Stillwater

Walking away from Holly was one of the hardest things I'd ever done. I'd rather tear my heart out than to watch her fall apart from my hurtful words, but I know what I did was right. My people would never take kindly to her as a potential wife of a chief, and her people would turn away from her and likely wish to execute her for being with the likes of me. I can't do it to her. No matter how much it hurts me. I've come to learn early that life can be cruel and unfair. This is one of those times. If only we could make this work. We met for a reason. Were we not destined to be with one another?

I stop outside my tepee and tilt my head up to the sky and cry out to the Great Spirit to ask why. Almost as soon as I do, I'm pulled back toward where I left Holly. Her sister, May, is screaming at her. She slaps Holly across the face as hard as she can. I can't interfere with their fight. I watch the girl I love sway on her feet to keep from falling to the ground, holding onto her face while her sister screams profanities about us. Further sealing my reasons for us being unable to stay together. Each word punches me in the gut and leaves me gasping for air. I can't seem to catch my breath. The grief is too strong. My feet are held to the spot. It's only when May leaves and Holly slumps to her knees that I run to her and gather her up in my arms, and she bawls against me like a baby. Maybe if I only hold her tight enough, all the hurt and pain that both May and I have thrown at her will keep her together. We stay sitting like this for what seems like hours.

Holly's tears turn to light snubs and disappear altogether. She's fallen asleep right here.

I do what I promised as a warrior I would never do. I cry until there are no more tears to shed. For tomorrow, I will lose my little dove forever, and with her, I will lose part of my heart.

Chapter 11

Holly

I startle awake, surprised to be lying on my pile of buffalo robes. It's dark outside, and everything is silent, signaling how late at night it is. I roll over and look at May's side of the tepee, but then do a double take.

"May?" Her bed is empty. Where could she have gone?

There, in the middle of her furs, is the little bear. The carving that Tall Bear gave to her was a peace offering after she'd first come here. She takes that little bear everywhere with her. Of course, she would never admit such a thing. Seeing it left behind gives me pause.

I lie still and wait, expecting that maybe she just went outside to relieve herself, but I wait, and then I wait some more, and I know something's not quite right.

I stand up slowly and tiptoe away, sidestepping White Deer, who sleeps very close to the door. She's a surprisingly heavy sleeper, but I still try to stay quiet.

I close the flap shut. "May?" I call out quietly, not expecting an answer. I don't get one. May had been acting strange earlier. I should have seen the signs that she wanted to run away. Now it's too late. Could she have gone toward the old cabin or toward the fort?

Panic claws up my throat. Either place is a bad idea. I can't believe she'd do something this stupid. Is it that bad living in this camp?

I take a step forward, and my foot lands in something wet. It's not raining. Why would the ground be wet? I stoop down to get a closer look. The moonlight shimmers over a red patch of liquid. It couldn't be anyone else's blood but May's.

I race toward Stillwater's tepee. If she's hurt, then I need him. He'll know what to do.

I pause outside, feeling unsure. "Stillwater?" I call. I refuse to barge in.

There's a light shuffle, and the flap is pulled back. "Holly?" He blinks as if unsure that I'm here. I take in his disheveled appearance, and if I wasn't in such a panic, I'd find this situation a little funnier.

"May is missing. I think she ran away. I found blood. She's hurt." My voice shakes, and I hate how frightened I sound. I'm worried that if May goes toward the cabin that she'll run into those wolves. She wouldn't survive such an attack. Her health is fragile enough after what she's gone through.

"I'll go to Tall Bear. He may know where she's gone." He takes my hand. "We'll find her. Try not to worry. I know it may be hard, but go back to your tepee. If White Deer finds you both gone, she will panic." He squeezes my hand and lets go.

I take a deep breath. "I'll try." I watch him depart and head toward Tall Bear's home. The moment I see Tall Bear poke his head out at the intruder bothering him at this time of night, I go back quietly.

THE WAY OF THINGS

I lie back down, but I don't go back to sleep. How can I? I pray that Tall Bear and Stillwater will find her in time.

Right before sunrise, Stillwater tells me Tall Bear is still looking. I left my bed of furs long ago. Unable to stand myself much longer, I sat outside against the tall oak right outside the edge of the village. As soon as it's light enough, I plan to make my own search if May isn't found.

I have no idea how Tall Bear can track her at all in the blackness of the night, but Stillwater always said he's the best tracker in the village. That and he and May are the closest among us all. I find it odd how she seems to confide in the giant Indian and not her own sister. Perhaps she thinks he is safer since he can't understand English. She keeps contradicting her loudly proclaimed hatred.

I would never tell her, but I suspect Tall Bear knows more English than he lets on. Even when he talks among his own people, he is very quiet.

Just when May seemed to be more comfortable here, she ran. It still makes no sense to me.

"He'll be back soon with your sister," Stillwater promises me. I'm not sure how he knows such a thing, but he sounds confident in his own words, whether he's being truthful or trying to keep me calm.

Nonetheless, not even a few hours after daylight, Tall Bear comes back on his horse with a ruffled looking May in front of him. She's not fighting to get away or angry. She is simply scared, clinging to Tall Bear's chest as if he's her lifeline. I don't notice at first until Tall Bear stops his horse and helps May down. Her legs give out from beneath her, and he catches her limp form.

I see the blood soaking the lower half of her dress. It coats her legs. Dried and new together. Her face is much too pale. I've seen this before on the wagon train. A woman who lost her baby and almost bled to death. I blanch, standing stock still and watching Tall Bear carry my sister away and into White Deer's tepee.

"Holly, your sister is hurt. She needs you." Stillwater touches my shoulder, and I blink. My feet drag in a sluggish daze until I'm at the entrance. How do I face May when I never knew she was with child? She kept it a secret and never thought to tell me. Outright refusing to tell me what was going on with her. I see it now. All those times she couldn't eat and was sick to her stomach. I thought it was simply all the trauma she endured, but it was much worse. I understand now the hate she's held inside herself all this time toward the people in this village. Hooked Nose had defiled her.

I turn away and take in a few gasps of calming breaths.

"Did you know your sister was with child?" Stillwater asks quietly, unable to read the turmoil brewing inside me.

"She never spoke a word of it."

A shadow falls over us in the entryway. "She told me, but I was sworn to secrecy." Tall Bear's voice joins us. He steps through and stands beside us, looking pale and haggard.

I careen my head up and meet his eyes. "You should have told me." May refused to tell me but told him everything? One of the very people she claimed to hate? I stumble back. I realize the small friendship I'd seen between them is so much more now. She'd told him all her secrets.

"She believed I couldn't understand her." Tall Bear shakes his head. "I know more words than many would believe." His words are pointed toward Stillwater, who stares at him in surprise. "It's easier to talk to someone when you think they can never tell another." Tall Bear hangs his head. "I'm sorry I said nothing. I believed she would tell her own sister in due time. My silence nearly cost her her life. She was my responsibility." Tall Bear closes his eyes and clenches his fists.

I'm about to say something else.

"Holly?" White Deer calls out to me from within.

"Coming!" I call back. I look back to Tall Bear. "I'm just glad we found her before it was too late. Thank you for finding her, Tall Bear." I reach out to squeeze his hand, but think better of it.

May is propped up into a sitting position when I step inside. She looks like she should lie down and rest, but she's wide awake, though more tired than I've ever seen her. She looks up at me when I sit down.

White Deer steps away to give us a little privacy and takes away the bloodied garments that May changed out of.

May bites her lip as if to keep back tears. "Can you please forgive me for keeping such a horrid secret from you? I didn't know what to do when I found out I was carrying *his* child. I thought if I said something, he might come back to drag me away. And I was"—she hiccups—"ashamed."

I take her hand. "I would never be ashamed of you. It wasn't your fault that he forced himself on you."

My words make her cry harder. "Can you forgive me for acting so terrible toward you and Stillwater? I'm a horrible person for casting blame where it doesn't belong." She squeezes my hand. "I treated him like dirt, and somehow he still treats me like I'm a precious pearl. I don't deserve his kindness. Did you know he gave Hooked Nose his prized horse just to save me? Oh Holly, that poor animal," May moans.

"Sssh. It's okay now." I wrap my arms around her gently and let her cry on my shoulder. She doesn't have to clarify who "he" is. I hide a smile. Perhaps it's the wrong time to be smiling, but I can't help it. For the first time, she's showing an emotion that doesn't involve hate, and that means she's healing.

Chapter 12

Holly

The silence is nearly deafening as we trudge toward the fort on horseback. I sit in front of Stillwater, who is deathly quiet. He won't listen to my pleas to stay in the village. Even if it's for May's sake, so she can rest. She's so weak, but she still insists we go. I can tell she can't wait to get away from this place. I can't blame her. She's been through too much. Was it just last night that she miscarried all alone in the woods? I'm still upset that she never told us she was with child. It didn't matter who the father was. She had nothing to be ashamed of; it never was her fault.

I didn't think the goodbyes between Stillwater and I would be so bitter, but here we are, right next to each other, and not saying a word. It's been hours since we left the village, and Fort Brigg's walls are visible now.

It's not my imagination that Stillwater's grip tightens around me the closer we get. He can say what he believes to be true, but I know he doesn't want to leave me here. It's his sense of duty that punishes us both.

Tall Bear carries May on his horse. She has long since caved into her fatigue. Her cheeks are paler than they should be, one side resting against Tall Bear, who keeps a careful grip to prevent her from slipping off. Despite being a very large, intimidating man, it seems with May he's more like a teddy bear, and I can't help but smile whenever I catch them together. May denies the visible attraction between them because of her prejudice, but I have a feeling that if she let herself forgive, she would find Tall Bear a fine candidate for a husband if we weren't both being left at this fort. At least May is happy about our situation. She is more than enough for the both of us, and it upsets me she doesn't see how torn Tall Bear is to see her go. It's such a shame. May is so close to accepting the people who helped her when she was in dire need, and now we'll see none of them again. Destined to set forth on a future wagon train. Destined to both marry men we will never love. Married to strangers. That ought to frighten May out of her wits after the ordeal she just went through.

I shiver at the bitter truth. A woman alone could never survive in this wilderness.

Stillwater touches my arm, and I nearly jump out of my skin after such a long length of silence. "Are you cold?"

"No. Just thinking about the future." I tell him the truth. I'm tired of making things up.

Just as he's about to ask another question, the relative quiet is disturbed. We look up. Soldiers on horseback head in our direction. May rouses, blinking at the commotion coming toward us. Her eyes widen at first, and then she relaxes at the sight of the soldiers.

I stiffen, remembering that we're two white women with two Indian warriors and how it might look to onlookers. What I don't expect is for one to hail Stillwater. They don't call him by name... They call him *halfbreed*.

I look up at him in shock, trying to see past those very native features, but I can't.

Stillwater gives the soldiers a salute, and all I can do is gape. Wondering what I've witnessed and wondering who Stillwater really is and what he hasn't told me about himself after I've told him everything about me. This revelation hurts worse than him telling me I needed to be with my kind... who was his kind?

I look toward May, and she looks at me in equal astonishment. Tall Bear's face is stoic. He doesn't seem surprised, which leads me to believe everyone knew Stillwater was half white all along. Everyone but me...

Tall Bear leans over toward Stillwater to say something. He doesn't seem very comfortable around so many soldiers. Glancing down at May with a torn expression, he says not a word to her, and she watches him dismount and hand her the reins.

"I will remember you." His English is heavily accented and broken, but he says it clearly and squeezes her hand. She stares down at him. Something shimmers in her eyes, and I know it's not a trick of the light. Tall Bear turns around and makes his way back the way we came.

I'm so lost in my thoughts that I miss going through the gate and, in a flash, we're dismounting. I blink at my surroundings. At first, I don't notice the familiar figure standing on the sidelines, watching me. Our eyes meet, and I stumble forward. Right into Stillwater's back.

"Adam?" I feel the color drain from my face, and I take a step back, away from him and away from Stillwater.

"Holly, I thought you were dead." He steps closer until he's right in front of me and Stillwater. He eyes the Indian in distaste.

I thought you were dead.

We assumed him dead, but here he is, standing right in front of me, and if I thought my existence was already looking dire now, I knew it could get much worse.

"Adam?!" It's May who speaks first. She steps in front of us, and I'm not sure of her reasonings, but I'm glad of her interference.

I press into Stillwater's side, and he looks down at me and then at Adam in confusion. "What is the matter?"

I open my mouth to explain, but Adam beats me to it and side steps May.

"I never thought I'd see my beloved fiancée again." He eyes Stillwater and then ignores him to take my hands. "Those Injuns murdered our entire wagon train before we made it to the fort. They thought they killed me, but I only pretended to be dead. I was sure they'd gotten to you and your grandmama." He squeezes my hands tightly. "I see they found you. Why ain't you dead?"

"No. I wasn't taken against m-my will," I stutter, looking toward May. Her face is a blank mask. She won't be helping me.

Adam doesn't listen to me, rounding on Stillwater. "Regardless of the situation, I am glad you're back. What is this Injun doing here, Holly? He hasn't hurt you, has he?"

My face burns because I realize Adam doesn't know that Stillwater can speak English, and if I don't say something quickly, then things could get out of hand.

I avoid Stillwater's gaze, but I can feel his eyes burning a hole into me. "Stillwater saved me, and I've stayed with his people until now. They've been nothing but kind. Please don't speak ill of them."

Adam scoffs. "It's okay to tell the truth."

I always knew he was unkind, but this was going too far, even for me. I pull my hands away from him in annoyance and sneak a glance at Stillwater. His expression is unreadable, unsuspecting, while he watches the soldiers walking about, looking like he wants to be anywhere but here. Who could blame him?

"Holly?" Adam sounds surprised I would react this way.

"I am here now. Let's leave everything in the past." I close my eyes and take a deep breath. Can I leave Stillwater in the past and never see him again? Can I truly do that? No, but I must...

"Adam!" someone calls, and he turns and hollers back. He looks back at me. "I need to go help a few soldiers with a few mules. I'll be back."

The three of us are left alone, and the silence is deafening. I dare to sneak a glance at Stillwater again, heat creeping up my face at his intent stare. I think I'm in this deep. Why hadn't I mentioned Adam at all? Well, in all fairness, I thought he was dead.

"What is a fiancée? I do not know that word." His question ties my stomach into knots, and I want so much not to have to tell him.

May beats me to it once again.

"Holly is arranged to marry Adam." She doesn't sugarcoat it, and I wince.

Stillwater looks stricken by her words, his brow furrowing in confusion.

"Our parents arranged for us to marry when we reached Oregon." I speak up, voice wavering. Things just keep getting more and more complicated. Is it too late to turn around and run in the opposite direction? I would rather stay in the old cabin than face his disappointment.

"It's none of my concern"—Stillwater meets my eyes—"who you marry." His gaze is soft. He's already forgiven me.

My heart breaks. We both know he doesn't mean it, but in the end, it won't matter after today.

With only a few more words between us, May and I watch Stillwater and Tall Bear leave, their backs to us. The gates close, and I flinch. May pulls my hand, and I turn to look at her, telling myself I won't cry.

"The colonel's wife wants to see us and help us to our room," May announces with another tug. I don't miss the stray tear she rubs from her face, but I say nothing. She's looking paler by the second. She needs rest.

Adam is coming back in our direction, and I pick up my steps. "Yes, let's go."

May's eyes dart toward Adam. "What is so horrible about Adam that you can't stand to be near him?"

I shake my head. She would never understand.

She scowls but stays silent, and we continue toward one of the larger of the crude, wooden buildings. Lifeless and void of color is my new existence.

We approach the main cabin and stop. Right before May raises her fist to knock, the door opens, and a woman with dark hair piled atop her head appears. Her dress is so full of lace that I'm taken aback.

"Hello girls, I'm Mrs. Stellar. I was told to expect you. Come in." She ushers us in, and suddenly, I feel so out of place and dirty. My deerskin dress is dusty and at odds with her satin and lace. May looks the same as me, but she looks a bit more at ease at her placement. Mrs. Stellar looks at me as if I'm something the dog dragged in, but her gaze toward May is much sweeter. I'm a tad miffed at the lady's attitude but keep a straight face.

Her first bit of business is getting two soldiers to bring in a hip bath, and a maid appears to pour hot water into it. May and I take turns in the tub. It's so strange to bathe in hot water again. I've gotten so used to the icy creek.

I try to compose my expression when May drops her doeskin dress on the floor of the cabin. I knew she was frail, but I didn't realize how much she'd changed since we were together with Ma and Pa. Her experience with the Indians differed greatly from mine. I can understand the pain she went through now. I know what exactly happened, but it's still such a hard thing to see your own sister standing there with scars up and down her arms and even her back and legs. They weren't there before, and she's lost so much weight.

"Staring is rude, you know." May's voice snaps me back into focus, and I flinch like a child caught with their hand in the cookie jar. She sinks into the water and furiously scrubs at the dust that accumulated over our ride. I can't help but wonder if she's scrubbing more than just the dirt.

I turn away and reluctantly remove the soft dress I've become accustomed to wearing. I can't say I'm happy about going back to itchy homespun once more. Let's not forget those petticoats. Maybe I can hold on to this doeskin dress a little while longer. With a sigh, I fold it and place it next to May's on a side table, which I'd also folded. I turn away to undo my braids.

"Could you hand me the soap?"

I drop my hair ties down beside the dresses and reach over to pick up the sliver of soap, handing it out toward May.

"Holly, you can't breathe a word about the baby." May shoots her hand out of the water to grab my arm instead of the soap.

I jerk back in surprise, and the soap plops into the bath. "Wh-what?" I'm shocked she's talking about this now out of nowhere. "If you so much as breathe a word about me birthing or carrying an Indian baby, I will be ruined, and there will be no hope of marrying a decent man here or in Oregon. Whichever might come first." Her breath catches. "No one will want a tainted woman."

Not a good one...

My eyes widen, knowing where this is heading. I squeeze May's hand and shake my head, but she keeps talking and doesn't pay attention to me.

"I'd have no way of supporting myself unless I—" her words break off in a sob. "I'd rather stay with the Lakota than become one of those women."

"No one will ever know, May." I try not to let her words rub me the wrong way. Becoming a prostitute was much worse than going back to the Lakota. How could anyone compare the two?

In my eyes, both of our futures are looking quite dim. I don't say what I'm thinking. Like that I was already destined to marry a man that wasn't considered 'good.' That we were both already sullied by being with the Lakota all this time...

I want to go back to Stillwater and his people already. How far did he and Tall Bear travel by now? Not far, I would think. If only I could step outside the gate and just leave this stuffy place. I don't belong here. But do I belong anywhere?

He doesn't want you, a little voice in my head calls out in a sing-song voice. I scowl at myself.

"I have prepared a meal for you." Mrs. Steller's voice carries over the dressing screen, and we both jerk in surprise. May nearly splashes water on the floor.

How long has the woman been there? Has she been listening long?

May shakes her head.

THE WAY OF THINGS

"Yes, Ma'am," I call out, and we hurriedly finish bathing.

To my chagrin, Mrs. Stellar pops herself behind the screen just as I'm dressing. I'm caught with my dress just over my head.

"Oh, no, dear girl," Mrs. Stellar says in horror. "You mustn't put that hideous, flea-bitten thing on again. You must wear this to be a proper lady." She shoves a practical, wool dress at me, complete with petticoats. It feels so heavy now that I'm not used to such things, but at least there's no lace dangling from the sleeves.

She hands another set to my sister, who doesn't say a word of complaint, and dresses happily as a white woman again. I don't miss the slip of her hand removing the little wooden bear from her other dress and tucking it into her itchy, cotton one. That bear means a lot to her. I wonder what would happen if someone knew who made it and tried to take it from her.

Mrs. Stellar, of course, is none the wiser and dismisses herself on the other side of the screen, demanding her maid take our old things and burn them out back.

Almost smugly, while no one is looking, I shove my feet back into my moccasins as an act of rebellion. If May can have Tall Bear's carving, then I can have my last reminder of Stillwater.

We step out.

Praising us as presentable, Mrs. Stellar guides us to a table that's too fancy to be in the likes of this fort. May and I sit, feeling rather awkward after sitting on the ground all this time.

Thus begins the beginning of our new life... as fort dwellers.

Chapter 13

Stillwater

Each thud of a hoofbeat sends a sharp pang to my chest. I feel wretched for leaving Holly in that place. It takes everything in me not to turn around and go back. But then I remember the man that called her his fiancée. His wife-to-be. She could never be mine if she was already someone else's. The best thing I can do now is let her go. She doesn't belong with me in this wild land. She belongs in a cabin with walls and a floor. With a white man, not a halfbreed like me.

"Stillwater?" Tall Bear pulls his horse in front of mine to stop me. "You should go back there and get her." I don't miss the underlying words he wishes to say. He misses May as much as I miss Holly.

"It's too late. She belongs there with them... with him."

The rest of our ride back is quiet.

When we reach the village, White Deer comes to find me and pushes me toward my father's tepee. "He wants to speak to you now," she says, as if it's urgent and cannot wait.

The moment I walk through the tepee flap, he berates me. "You have gone and done something rash again."

I'm confused. "What do you mean? I took the sisters back to where they belong."

"You took them back to where YOU thought they belonged. Did you ever stop and ask the girl what she wanted? She has no home or people and was happy here. I would have allowed her to stay and be adopted into our village. Her and her sister both. Being white has nothing to do with whether or not they belong. After all, you belong here just as much as they do."

I open my mouth, but nothing comes out. He's right, and I can find no argument to speak of. I sit heavily on the furs across from him, my heart heavy in my chest. "I think I made a mistake."

My father scoffs. "I'm glad you can admit it. Now you must fix it."

"What?" Does he really want me to go back and get them after I dropped them off? "I thought you wanted me to take them back there."

"I never said that, son. You assumed I did and never asked." He stands over me, and I feel like a little boy being scolded all over again.

I hang my head. "I didn't want to leave Holly. She's marrying one of the men there, and I'm afraid he's more than a little cruel."

"If you love her, then you must go after her and bring her back before it's too late." He claps me on my shoulder in finality.

I nod and stand up. "I'll take Tall Bear with me."

"The men at the fort may not let you take the sisters peacefully."

I know this well, and I can only hope for the best.

Holly

Two days pass after Stillwater and Tall Bear leave us at the fort. Not a moment has gone by that I haven't wanted to turn tail and run back to the Lakota village, but unfortunately, there's not a way to leave, and Adam has become like a burr stuck to my side at all hours of the day unless he has to step away to help the men with the horses or heavy lifting. I've noticed he doesn't do much since he's been in this fort, at least not since I've arrived. My Pa would call him lazy. If he were here now to see the man he wanted me to marry, would he still believe him to be a decent husband? When he's not busy doing odds and ends, he's nursing a bottle.

I scoff at the thought, scrubbing the cup in my hands harder than necessary. Even May, who at first couldn't understand my reasonings for not wanting to marry the man, is slowly changing her tune by the hour, since she's the other burr on my side that won't leave. She's the only welcomed burr, of course.

I dread the days and months that will stretch on until we meet another wagon train heading toward Oregon.

These dreary walls that surround the simple, wood cabins feel like a jail cell. I miss the green, lively trees, but here, all to see are dead ones constructed as buildings. Perhaps I've lived with the Indians too long to appreciate a cabin now. They make me feel so confined.

Now marks the end of our second day. The sun is sinking low on the horizon.

May sits quietly on her single straw-filled mattress bed. The ropes beneath it creak and groan. She's quiet. Too quiet. She's thinking about the same things I am. Her situation and the life she left behind. No matter what she says, I know she misses her time with the Lakota. She made another life there, and Tall Bear cared for her a great deal in his quiet way. Everyone noticed but her. It doesn't matter now.

I sigh. Her coloring has at least improved with much needed rest.

The bed creaks. "Could you please stop sighing?" May grumbles.

Before I can reply, there's a sharp tap on the door, and we both startle in surprise. I set the cup back into the basin I'm using to wash dishes and step toward the door. I barely open it up before Adam is pushing his way inside.

My nose curls when he steps past me. The stench of whisky is strong on his breath. I keep myself a few strides behind him as he makes himself comfortable on one of the rough-hewn kitchen chairs. It wobbles beneath his weight until he plants his feet down on the dirt floor.

He looks toward May. "Can I have a word with your sister in private?" It's an order disguised as a question, but she gets up, giving me a questioning look.

"If you insist." She gives him a small glare and saunters away from us.

I shrug, trying to look nonchalant. An uneasy feeling makes itself at home inside my stomach.

"The colonel will marry us tomorrow," Adam announces as May slips out of the room to give us privacy. I wish she had stayed. Adam stumbles toward me. The smell of his breath brings bile to my throat, but I stand my ground.

"Marry us?" The words come out of me in a stutter. Somewhere in the back of my mind, I thought since both our parents were dead, the marriage would fall through, but apparently he thought not.

"It's what our Mas and Pas wanted. We should honor their wishes." Adam takes another step toward me, and I take one back.

Too late, I realize my skirt is not straightened and one of my moccasins is peeping out from beneath the hem. I tug quickly, but his eyes have already caught sight of my little rebellion. I babble to change his focus. "No, Adam. I can't marry you. Least of all... not now." I never wanted to marry him, and now I can't stomach the thought.

"Can't or won't?" His face turns red in anger. I can see his father in him, remembering Grandmama's words about the apple not falling far from the tree, and I know I've made the right choice. Even if no one can understand.

"I can't marry you. I don't love you, and I never will."

"You're in love with that Injun." He glares down at me, hate filling his eyes. He doesn't understand anything.

I can't answer him. If I do, he'll be even angrier. I step closer to the door, inch by inch, hoping he doesn't notice.

Adam continues to rage on and doesn't seem to realize that I haven't said a word. "Your head has always been full of fanciful things. Always in them clouds. Don't you know there ain't no such thing as love in this world? It's all about survival. That's all that matters, Holly." He advances toward me, and I shrink back. "You think that Injun loves you?" He laughs, and it makes the hair on the back of my neck rise. Adam raises his hand. "Didn't your Pa tell you not to trust them heathens?" He slaps the side of my face. "That was for your Pa, and this one's for me." My head snaps to the side with the second blow, and my cheek pulsates in pain. "I won't allow you to have eyes for no Injun. You hear me? And you will marry me!" Adam shouts. His eyes are wild and unhinged, like the wolf that attacked me. I can no longer shrink away from him, my back slamming against the door to the small cabin. Adam grabs my shoulders and shakes me like a rag doll. "Them Injuns killed everyone!" He wraps his hands around my neck and squeezes. I feel the door digging into my back. I— I can't breathe.

I attempt a breathy scream and try to get away, but that only makes him that much angrier.

"You shut up, you little wench!" He shoves me, and I lose my balance, slamming my head into the corner of the table. It isn't enough for him to see me bleed. He lifts his foot and slams his heavy boot into my stomach.

"Adam, p-please stop," I whimper, trying to curl into a ball to protect myself. Blood runs down my forehead and drips to the dirt floor.

"I bet you let that savage lay his hands on you, didn't you?!"

He kicks me again, sending me rolling across the floor, and I try to speak before Adam issues another blow. "No, Adam, it's not like that."

"But it is!"

The door bangs open, and May stares between us in horror. Me on the floor, bleeding out; Adam staring back in anger. "Get away!" May yells. Stepping into the small room, she advances on Adam. "Don't you dare touch my sister!" She swings her little fist at him, and it connects across his jaw. He takes a step back and shakes his head, holding the side of his face as if he can't seem to imagine why May would hit him. He shakes his head once more, and his foggy eyes look clearer.

His eyes widen at me on the floor. "Holly?" He reaches for me.

With a painful roll and a flip, I push my abused body to stand up and stumble to stand by May. "Don't touch me!"

"Adam, it's time for you to leave," May growls. "Holly will be ready to marry you tomorrow."

"May, wh—?" she hushes me, and I clamp my lips shut. I try to clear my head, but my vision is so fuzzy, and everything seems to spin around, so I stop and simply hold my head with one hand. The other holds onto May before the floor comes up to greet me.

Adam stares at me, as if he can't believe that he just beat me, but doesn't dare open his mouth again. He slips out the door without a word.

May latches the door behind him with a sound thump and whirls back to me. "He almost killed you!" I expected one of her sour expressions, but what I didn't expect was the tears in her eyes. I don't have time to say another word before she gathers me into her arms and hugs me. I want to tell her it hurts, but I can't bring myself to do so when this is the first hug I've received from my sister in months.

And there, May breaks down and cries like a baby. Everything that we went through in the last few months comes out in a rush. "Holly, I'm so sorry. I never understood why you disliked Adam so much and never stopped to listen to your reasons. Now I've gotten us stuck in this horrible place. We know no one but Adam, and he's proven never to be trusted again."

"May, it's all right. You didn't know how this would turn out." She helps me sit down in a rocking chair, and the dizziness recedes for a moment. May presses a cloth to my forehead to staunch the bleeding. It's not as bad as it looks... At least, that's what I'm hoping for.

"We should have stayed at the Indian village. We almost had a home there with White Deer and the others." May sniffs, her voice lowering. "Stillwater cared for you a great deal. He would never have treated you like Adam did. I think I'm ashamed of talking so badly about him and the people in the village. They weren't the ones that killed Ma and Pa and were so kind to us. All I did was treat them nasty." She hangs her head. "I'm so ashamed, Holly. Tall Bear was nothing but kind to me."

"May, I forgive you, and I know they forgive you. You suffered a great deal and didn't know who to trust." I lift a clean part of the hem of my dress and dab at her eyes. "It's over and done now. We have to make the best of things." My words are confident, but inside, there's an inferno of fear and insecurity of what tomorrow will bring and the new chapter of my life that will begin with it. I wish tomorrow would never come.

She looks up at me, and I'm taken aback by her flashing, determined gaze. "I want to go back."

"We can't." Could we? "They'll never let us leave here. Especially Adam. He's made himself our guardian."

"You can't marry him. I'll be next, and who knows who Adam will pick for me to marry. He'll have control over me as my brother-in-law." May is insistent. "We must leave tonight. It's the only way."

"That's crazy. We don't even have horses or anything stored up to take with us." She's talking nonsense. How can we pull this off? Oh, but I want to do just what she says.

We don't see Adam again after he leaves our cabin, and May and I try to pack some bread and cheese that we had left over from supper.

My body is sore, and I'm not so sure that one of my ribs isn't cracked, but if we don't go now, then there will never be another chance to run away again. My head is still pounding, and one of my eyes is almost swollen shut. I must look like a sight.

It's so dark outside that we can barely see anything. I'm so afraid that we can never pull this off. May's idea is crazy, but it just might work. She wants to distract the guards at the gate by opening the corral and releasing all the horses. I pray everything will go as planned, or we could be in some serious trouble.

I hold our sack of precious items and hide in the shadows, watching as May walks with the slyness of an Indian. Where did she learn to be so silent? She creeps up to the corral and unlatches it, sprinting toward me and ducking down. We watch as, one by one, the horses spill out in a great frenzy.

The two guards make a frantic attempt to push them back. One by one, people open their cabin doors to see what all the fuss is about.

Here's our chance, while the gate is unguarded. We can't open the gate all the way, so we have to slip out through a tiny space. The hardest part is the board that keeps the enormous doors closed. We both push on it to get it to move, and it makes a horrible screech. We pause for a good few seconds, but none of the men or soldiers pay us any mind because the horses are so loud. And then we slip through.

THE WAY OF THINGS

We are free but have a long walk to our destination. If we make it, it may be a miracle. We have no further choice but to push on and hope for the best. Without horses, it will take us much longer, and neither of us are fit for a trek in the wilderness. At least winter has not set in just yet. The cold stings our cheeks, but as long as we keep moving, we will be warm enough.

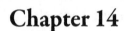

Chapter 14

Holly

We stumble on tired and cramping feet, forcing ourselves to put one foot in front of the other. I feel close to passing out, but I know we have to make more ground before daylight. At our rate, it'll take us three nights to get back to the village, and every moment will count. We'll have to sleep during the day and stay hidden. At the moment, we're still in danger of being caught. So far, no one has taken notice of two women missing from their cabin... not yet. When they do, I'm sure it will be Adam who notices first since he planned to marry me the next day.

I shiver at how close I was to becoming that man's wife.

I'm thankful that my injuries don't affect my walking because we're making good time already.

Hours later, the daylight threatens to peak over the horizon, and we quickly make a lean-to to cover us in a cove of bushes. It will have to do, and even though I have a rock under my back, I'm too tired to care. I long for my buffalo robes in White Deer's tepee. I long for White Deer's company. The older woman was so dear to us. So much like a younger version of Grandmama. It isn't just Stillwater that I miss, although he is the one I miss the most.

THE WAY OF THINGS

We force ourselves to stay quiet and rest until the next nightfall, then we travel again.

At first, traveling isn't so bad. On the first day, it's only the slightest discomfort. Perhaps the adrenaline has me going full force. We're so focused on putting distance between us and the fort. By the second day, my side makes itself known by hurting so much I find difficulty doing the easiest tasks. I know I'm hurting myself further. I have a cracked rib, and I'm aggravating it. However much it hurts, I know I can't stop walking. What waits back at that fort is much worse than the pain I'm putting myself in.

So, on we walk, and in comes the third day. The end of our miserable journey and the beginning of a new one.

May and I are making meals out of edible plants.

We're picking berries when we hear a noise in the distance. It gets louder and louder, and we realize at the same time that horses approach.

I drop my handful of berries in the folds of my dress. "May! Someone's coming!" I yank my sister behind a gigantic oak tree.

"Ouch!" she grumbles, but otherwise stays quiet. We listen to the hoofbeats vibrating the earth. Two horses appear in our view, the riders visible. Two Indian men pushing their steeds at full speed.

I gasp and drop away from the tree. "Stillwater!"

Both horses slide to a stop, and the Indian with the flyaway hair freezes and stares toward me like he can't believe I'm actually here and calling after him.

I don't waste any time. I sprint toward him, my side pitching a fit, but I refuse to let it stop me.

Stillwater dismounts from his horse and grabs me in his arms.

A squeak of pain escapes me as he squeezes me in a hug. It's too tight. He recoils and sets me down, realizing something is wrong. He frowns when he catches sight of me. My black eye, the bruises on my arms, and the gash on my forehead.

"He's hurt you." Stillwater is unhappy. His fingers gently push back the hair from my face. "How could a man who wishes to marry you be so cruel?" he says under his breath.

"I'm all right, now." I take his fretting hands and squeeze them in mine.

His brow furrows, anger sparking in his eyes, and I'm taken aback by the intensity. I've never seen him so upset before. Not once. "I will kill him."

"No, Stillwater. He's not worth it."

He closes his eyes and takes a deep breath. "If he comes near you again, I'll—" His fists clench.

"No, the revenge is all mine," May insists, butting into our conversation.

"No killing and no revenge!" I chastise them both, looking over at Tall Bear, who stands between us three, looking lost.

Stillwater keeps an arm around my shoulders to keep me anchored, as if he thinks I'll disappear once more, and leads me toward his horse. "We must ride," he tells Tall Bear in Lakota.

I'm proud of myself for knowing enough words to follow through a conversation. He sets me on the front of his black horse and leaps up behind me. May mounts up Tall Bear's newly adopted white pony, and we're off.

"We escaped the fort to come back to the village. I want to stay," I say nervously, fingers gripping Stillwater's wrists.

He peers down at me. "I was coming back to take you home."

I look up at him in shock. "Home?" The word sounds so sweet on his lips. A warmth spreads across my chest at such a notion. I hadn't had a home in so long. To have a home once again... Being there in that village with Stillwater, White Deer, and even the others was like being home.

"You belong in that village as much as I do." He presses a kiss on the top of my head. "I'm so sorry I ever doubted that. My father had many words to say about my rash decisions."

"You mean that? Chief Strong Wind will let May and I stay?" I nearly forget that I'm sitting astride a horse, trying to turn to look at Stillwater fully in the face. I gasp as I nearly unsettle myself. My ribs protest.

"Stay!" The words fly out of his mouth, and I'm reminded of the day I woke up and he forced me to lie still. The words are almost funny now. His arms wrap around me tightly, and I gasp again, but this time in pain. "Ouch!"

There he goes once more, frowning. I think I've ruined the moment with my clumsiness.

"I—I mean..." I don't know what to say to him. He doesn't know the extent of my injuries. It's enough that he's seen my bruises. He's angry already. There's no need to put any more fuel on the fire. He might hightail it back to the fort and fight Adam. I can't let that happen. They would likely try to hang him on the spot for assault on a white man.

Just the thought sends a chill down my back. In the end, I don't tell him for his own sake. I fall asleep not long after, and it could have been an hour or a day before we reached the village, and I wouldn't have known.

Light seeping from the ceiling causes me to peel my eyes open, but it's the chirping birds and crackling fire that has me snapping awake.

I shoot forward and hiss in pain, flopping backward with a gasp and ungraceful plop.

"Holly?" a familiar voice calls my attention. May and White Deer sit beside me.

My surroundings make more sense. I'm in a tepee—not in the shack house at the fort.

"White Deer!" I'm speaking in Lakota before even realizing it. The language is now as easy as English. "I've missed you so much. I–I never thought I'd see any of you again." And then the tears begin, and I'm wiping them off one at a time, but they just keep coming.

White Deer pulls me into her small but strong arms. "I know, child. I know." Somehow, we all three cry in earnest. Each realizing we never wish to say goodbye ever again. Even May, who had once resented being here, is hugging White Deer.

"Now." White Deer pulls away and gives us a stern but playful smile. "No more tears."

They help me prop myself up and leave to tend to a few chores, claiming to come back with some roasted fish for me. Just the mention of food that doesn't consist of berries and basically weeds has my stomach growling.

Almost as soon as the two leave, someone else pops their head inside the tepee.

Stillwater.

I smile and open my mouth to call out to him, but he's not alone. Healing River steps out from behind him, and he's holding his famous smoking herbs.

I gag. By now, the man should know not to bring that stuff near me.

The medicine man gives me a big smile. It's unnerving because I almost never see him smile. Is it just me, or is he holding those stinky herbs closer than necessary?

I give another hack and wince at my throbbing side.

Stillwater frowns and whispers something to Healing River. I strain to hear and silently huff when I can't.

The other man nods and steps out with his herbs. The air soon clears, and I take a few gulps of fresh air in appreciation. I glare after Stillwater's teacher. I think he enjoys choking me out on purpose because the man doesn't like me, and I cannot fathom why. People either love me in this village or hate me. There seems to be no in between.

Stillwater sits on his knees beside me. "You've been asleep for three days. Are you feeling better?"

Three days?! How could I sleep for so long?

A frown covers his usual pleasant expression, and I'm taken aback. I thought he'd be a little more happy, but I'm mistaken. Before I can ask what's wrong, he's already speaking.

"You never mentioned how bad you were hurt." His hands clench into fists in his lap.

I glance down from his accusing gaze. It's true that I didn't tell him. "I didn't want to upset you."

"It was too late for that when I saw the bruises and your busted lip."

He has a fair point.

"I'm sorry." I stare down at his hands to avoid his eyes.

"I'm thankful he didn't hurt you any more than he did." His frown deepens. "I left you there, and I'm so sorry for it."

"It's not your fault," I try to argue.

Stillwater gives a self-deprecating laugh. "I never told you, but I'm sure you figured it out at the fort that I'm a half-breed. I'm not the chief's son by blood. He found me and my mother abandoned by my white father, alone and near death. He took us in and married my mother, adopting me. I hate that about myself. I loathe the white man for what he's done to the land and to my people, but how can I do that without hating myself? My feet are straddling different worlds"

"There are bad people in this world, and it has nothing to do with what color your skin is. Please don't talk badly about the person I love most."

Stillwater stares at me with wide eyes but doesn't have time to answer back. May steps through the entrance with a bowl of steaming food. "I know I promised roasted fish, but Rising Sun offered a bowl of her deer stew, and I hear it's famous." She doesn't look up from staring at the bowl that's filled so high to the brim it's threatening to spill over. She stops in front of me and looks up. "Oh!" Her face turns red, and you would think the two of us were up to no good instead of innocently sitting beside each other. Perhaps it's the intense look Stillwater wears on his face from my confession.

I pat a spot beside me. "Thank you, May."

She shuffles forward. I forget May is still skittish around men.

Stillwater scoots back, sensing her discomfort. She hands me the bowl.

I take a careful sip. The savory meat broth tickles my taste buds. As much as I hate to admit it, Rising Sun is a really wonderful cook.

"Rising Sun doesn't mind that I'm eating her stew?" I raise an eyebrow at May.

She shrugs.

What a rascal my sister is.

Stillwater snickers beside me. Watching him laugh, May relaxes ever so slightly. She's come such a long way since she first arrived in the village.

"Rising Sun is not so bad once you get to know her, you know." May's words are pointed at me.

I lower the bowl from my lips in quiet shock. Don't tell me that the two of them are becoming friends. I don't know if I can handle that. As soon as the thought crosses my mind, I feel ashamed of myself. Perhaps I shouldn't think so harshly of her. After all, I came here and took Stillwater's attention off of her. Even if it wasn't intentional... It still happened. She sees me as a threat. I never meant to be one.

"If you say so," I grump and go back to sipping the stew I'm undeniably enjoying.

I can feel Stillwater's gaze as I finish the bowl and ask for seconds with a sheepish look. It's really a ruse to get May to leave because if I don't get her out soon, I think Stillwater will drill a hole in my head with all his staring.

May smiles and tells us she'll be back. She takes her time.

Stillwater immediately sits beside me when May's footsteps fade. "The one you love most?"

My cheeks burn, meeting his eyes. "You've been here for me through the thick and thin of it all. How can I not love you?"

Stillwater heaves a long sigh, and at first, I think he's disappointed with my feelings, but then he smiles. "Thank the Great Spirit. I thought you would never admit it."

He presses his lips to mine, and I don't get another word in.

Chapter 15

Holly

Three months come and go and, with it, the cold season, or winter, as we call it. A lot happened during that time.

May and I became part of the tribe, embracing the Indian way and shedding the rest of our past. We had a clean slate, and we were both eager to put what happened at the fort behind us.

Stillwater began courting me as Indian couples do, and it wasn't long before he asked me to marry him. We prepared to have our own tepee and planned to marry as soon as spring came. There was a lot to prepare. It seemed fitting to marry instead of searching for a family to adopt me in. White Deer took May in as her new daughter without a second thought.

May and Rising Sun became fast friends. They were such an unlikely pair. At first, it was hard to wrap my head around the two. They seemed to soften each other up. May needed a friend, so I forced myself to like Rising Sun. It didn't take long before my pretending became real.

She must have forgiven me for taking Stillwater away from her. She never mentioned her upset again.

While Stillwater and I were preparing a future together, May and Tall Bear finally stopped tip-toeing around each other and began courting. It was about time. I couldn't be any happier about it. Never did two people go together more.

Stillwater and I married on the first day of the season. There was dancing and feasting and everyone celebrated with us. Even the ones who didn't like me. They were happy for Stillwater. It was the happiest day of my life, and I would treasure it always.

THE FIRST WARM DAY, Stillwater and I set out to forage for any remaining herbs that had survived the cold winter. We're running low on things, and the villagers are asking Stillwater for more of his seemingly famous medicine.

I'd shadowed my husband more than once on his visits to the sick. The medical knowledge of these people is fascinating, almost as fascinating as the man teaching me.

Healing River announced before Stillwater and I married that his time as the shaman was ending and gave Stillwater most of his patients. I was happy to stay away from him and his smoking herbs.

Chief Strong Wind gave up trying to talk his son out of dabbling in medicine, relenting at Healing River's public announcement. It wasn't an option to tell his son he couldn't take up Healing River's legacy. The people would have been outraged. Someone had to take care of them, and Stillwater was the only one leading the path of a medicine man.

So, it was settled just like that. The day of our wedding, Stillwater became the new Medicine Man and my husband.

"Holly?" My name pulls me from my thoughts, and I look up from my futile attempt at pulling up the straggling weed-like plant in my fingers. I've yanked the leaves from the stem—oops.

"Do you hear that?" Stillwater stills; as straight as the trees surrounding us. I hear absolutely nothing, but I don't tell him so. He has the ears of an eagle and the eyes to match.

Then I hear it. It's soft at first, but distinctly like thunder, and since there's no hint of rain in the air, it can't be. I look up to peer through the trees, but it's useless to see through the density.

"Someone's coming to the village." Stillwater stuffs the rest of his foraged goods into the pouch hanging on his belt and turns toward me. His eyes are alight with urgency.

"Is it another band of warriors with more captors?" I straighten from my stoop, abandoning my efforts.

He takes me by my hand. "No, it's a single horse, and not an Indian pony." He doesn't wait for me to answer and pulls me down the small hill with its lovely trees.

My belly takes a nosedive. A white man on a horse. No. It couldn't be.

The creek greets us next, but we don't stop. Stillwater continues to pull me on our way back down to the village. His hand is firm but gentle. I know I should trust him, but I have such an awful feeling. I'm not so sure I want to go back to the village yet.

The closer we get, the louder the hoofbeats become until they're a roar. The roar competes with my heart, which insists on galloping right along with the horse that's charging for our little camp at full speed.

A scout gives off a warning call.

"Whatever you do, Holly, stay close until we know what this newcomer wants," Stillwater warns. There's an underlying distress in his voice. He doesn't have to tell me who has come because I already know.

By the time we reach the tepees, the rider has approached us.

Adam holds a rifle in his hands, and his gaze meets Stillwater's. Stillwater glares back, tensing beside me. We stop a few yards in front of my former fiancé. Familiar faces spill out from their tepees. Chief Strong Wind and his sister. May and Tall Bear and the others. They run toward us, and I panic.

"No, Stillwater!" I yank against his grasp in horror. I don't want to be closer. I want to go back to the forest. This can't be happening! Stillwater holds fast, pushing me behind him, trusting that I won't run away. And I won't. Not without him.

"What's the matter, Holly? Didn't think I could find ya?" Adam spits from his perch, waving the firearm wildly in an arch over his head. His words are slurred. Not that of a drunk man but of a man who hasn't slept in days. A man who has gone off the deep end. His eyes are bloodshot and wild, darting between Stillwater and me as if he can't decide on who to look at. But then his eyes fasten on me once more, peeking behind Stillwater. I don't make a move to step forward.

"Ain't that cozy. You get kidnapped by Indians. The same ones who murdered our families. You're returned to me and then run straight back here again. You and your sister both," Adam hisses at me, and his horse takes a sidestep, shivering from his angry master.

"They weren't the ones who killed them and you know it." May seethes at his words, stepping toward him, but Tall Bear holds her back with a shake of his head.

"They're all the same. Get away from that savage, Holly. I've come to take you back. And I only have room for one of you." Adam slides down with a stagger and takes a step toward us. "I only prefer to take back my wife. I won't touch the soiled goods." The spurn is thrown toward May.

My sister turns ashen in shock. No one is supposed to know about the baby. How could he have known? Unless Mrs. Stellar overheard us...

Tall Bear growls and makes a move toward Adam, but both May and Chief Strong Wind yank him back just in time. It takes a lot of effort to keep the giant of a man in place. He stills but trembles in his rage. No one can stop him from glaring.

"You can't take Holly. She is now Lakota and my wife," Stillwater says quietly, without a stutter.

"I guess that settles that, then." He laughs, and it's a horrible, hollow sound that rings through the valley. "We can't have that now, can we?

I hold my breath and watch in horror as Adam's grip on the rifle tightens. Everything happens so fast. There's no time to react.

There's a quiet moment as Adam raises the rifle. The sort of quiet that comes right before something terrible happens, where the air rings and your life seems to flash before your eyes, and then everything comes to focus.

Stillwater shoves me hard away from him, and I hit the ground with a thud that echoes the gunshot that rends the air.

"Stillwater!" I scream and watch as the bullet buries itself into my husband's side and he crumbles to the ground only a few feet away.

"No!" There's another scream, and I barely register that it's my own. I try to crawl toward him.

A boot presses into my forearm. Pain shoots upward, making me lightheaded. "Holly, you should have listened. If I can't have you, then he can't, either. You'll be alone." He laughs again, and I know he's gone, the way he rambles on. He presses down harder when I try to wiggle away. I reach for Stillwater to staunch the blood flow and cry when I can't reach him.

In an instant, Adam is pulled away, and he screams profanities at Tall Bear, who yanks him away from me.

Dragging myself, I make it to Stillwater and press my hand on the hole that's been ripped through him. The blood seeps through my fingers. There's too much of it.

Tall Bear is distracted for only a second at the sight of Stillwater's blood, but that second is all it takes for Adam to rip away from him and point the rifle to his own throat.

"There's nothing else I can do now." Adam cackles. Tall Bear lunges for him once again to rip the gun out of his grip, but he's too late as another shot rings out. Adam falls to the ground on his knees. His eyes focus on me, and I watch the light bleed out with the blood that pours from the hole he blew through himself. He falls face first into the dirt.

I rip my eyes away. I can't look anymore, or I think I'll fall apart. None of this is real, I try to tell myself. My arm throbs, but my heart throbs more with pain.

Tall Bear is beside me, beside his friend. "I must get him to Healing River." He pries my hands away. I fall back and wipe them on the ground to remove the red that stains them. I think I'm going to be sick. I gasp for air and am only vaguely aware of White Deer and May guiding me away from the bloody scene in front of my eyes. Ahead, Tall Bear carries an unconscious Stillwater toward Healing River's tepee. He looks so much smaller, and frail, in the bigger man's arms. I try to focus on that instead of the blood continuously blooming, a growing red patch on his deerskin shirt.

"It's going to be all right, Holly," May says shakily, but even she can see how dire the situation has become.

"Adam is dead." My voice is flat, lifeless.

May squeezes my hand. "He'd been through so much horror, it made him crazy. He didn't know what he was doing."

"Yes, he did!" Anger surges through me. How could anyone justify killing? He would have killed me had Stillwater not stepped in. He would have killed both of us in a jealous rage.

"Let the good Lord judge that sorry man. There's nothing to be done about what happened now. We must concentrate on Stillwater." May is right. Bless the girl for blatantly ignoring the fact that apparently more than us knew about what happened to her during her captivity.

White Deer begins to cry in earnest, following closely behind Tall Bear. Other women and children creep from their tepees with the passing danger. Some join White Deer and cry with her. The piercing sounds feel like knives digging into me, and suddenly, I want to escape as much as I want to be by Stillwater's side. My chest tightens, and I try to draw in a shaky breath.

When we reach Healing River's tepee, the former shaman comes out as if waiting. I'm sure he heard the gunshots. He ushers Tall Bear in with him and tells the rest of us to wait outside.

Chief Strong Wind is next to arrive and doesn't wait to ask to go inside to see his son.

I step forward, intent on joining him. I have a right to see my husband, don't I?

White Deer pulls me back. "No, child. You must wait here. That is no place for a woman. We should see to your arm."

A wail of my own escapes me. "My arm is fine. Just a little bruised." I blubber the rest of my words. I take a deep breath but can't seem to find enough air.

"Holly, you need to breathe," May tells me.

130

THE WAY OF THINGS

Stillwater's pained scream is my undoing.
Darkness edges my vision, and the ground rushes to my face.

Chapter 16

Holly

Something touches my forehead, and I furrow my brow. Trying to gather my surroundings, I blink my eyes. I'm in an unfamiliar tepee. I turn my head to see a pair of groggy eyes staring back at me.

"Stillwater?" I ask, and shoot up in shock. My eyes rove over him, inspecting his injuries. A cloth is wrapped around his middle, hiding evidence of any wounds. Other than the ghostly-white sheen on his face, Stillwater looks well, and if I hadn't seen him shot, I would be second guessing if it even happened... but it did. I swallow back the tears threatening to burst forth once again.

"I heard you fainted and became another patient." The joke falls flat and definitely never reaches his eyes.

"I thought Adam killed you." I force my voice from shaking like a leaf. My tears find their escape and drip down my nose, and I lay down beside him and face him.

"I did too." Stillwater hums. "Better me than you."

"He wanted to kill us both, but he didn't."

"He was too far gone to know what he was doing. Men will go crazy after something as traumatic as seeing their family slaughtered in front of them." He wipes my cheek with a finger.

THE WAY OF THINGS

"Adam shot himself." I should feel more relief than I do, but all I can see when I close my eyes is him shooting himself over and over, and the blood. There was so much blood. More blood than what covered Stillwater.

"Tall Bear told me." Stillwater frowns, closing his eyes. "They may come looking for him."

"They?" I raise my head and peer down at him. He opens his eyes.

"Some men at the fort may come looking for Adam when he doesn't come back. It seems odd that he came alone."

"Maybe he just left without telling anyone. He's always been prideful and refused help," I supply, but unease lingers behind hours later.

Hours trickle into days, and there's no sign of anyone coming to avenge Adam's death. From what I'd seen at the fort, he wasn't very well liked, and likely everyone was relieved when he left. It took a while before I stopped looking over my shoulder, waiting for someone to drag me back to the fort. Fortunately, no one bothered us. I know that the day will come when things will change; good change or bad. The world is changing, and the settlers are coming in droves. For now, all is well.

When Stillwater is well again, he takes up his task as Medicine Man in great stride until Healing River stops accompanying him. I become his assistant whenever I'm needed. We make a great team, he and I.

Every night I go to sleep, I look up through the smoke hole of the tepee at the twinkling stars and remember the words Grandmama spoke and smile.

She wanted me to marry for love, and I have. I'd like to think she would have liked Stillwater if she'd gotten to know him.

"Stare at the stars as much as you want, but you will never count them all." A teasing voice tickles my ear.

I turn my head toward Stillwater and give him a playful thump on the nose.

I place my hand on the roundness of my stomach. "I can't sleep."

Stillwater places his hand over mine. "Be still, little one."

I laugh at his efforts and know it's useless, but I wouldn't trade this moment for anything. I can't imagine being anywhere but right here in this Lakota village, married to this man. Though it makes me sad that my family is gone, I'll never forget them. I still have May. The people of this village have become my new family. It's the way of things and new beginnings, and I plan to make the most of it.

I press a kiss to Stillwater's lips. "Thank you."

In the moonlight, he looks puzzled. "For what?"

"For being you."

Don't miss out!

Visit the website below and you can sign up to receive emails whenever Emma Rose Lee publishes a new book. There's no charge and no obligation.

https://books2read.com/r/B-A-TWWU-DMSAC

BOOKS 2 READ

Connecting independent readers to independent writers.

About the Author

Emma Rose Lee has been scribbling since she was seven years old and writes inspirational historical romance. She loves Native American History, cats, classic BBC movies, and Happily Ever Afters. She lives in North Carolina and when not writing, can be found playing Howrse, reading a good book on her kindle, or daydreaming.

Read more at https://www.amazon.com/author/emmaroselee.

CPSIA information can be obtained
at www.ICGtesting.com
Printed in the USA
LVHW020544121022
730468LV00014B/423

9 798215 453862